Praise for the Odessa

"It's been a treat to watch Wesley [...] cozier and more paranormal-ting[...] [...] began last year with *A Glimmer of Death* and continues now with *A Fatal Glow*, featuring the sleuthing adventures of the Realtor-turned-caterer Odessa Jones." —*The New York Times Book Review* on *A Fatal Glow*

"There's crispness in Wesley's plotting and sparkle in the supporting characters, notably Dessa's feisty, elderly aunts—both possessed of extrasensory gifts—and a possible love interest in ex-cop Lennox Royal. There's also something oddly comforting about a Black woman in fiction who isn't weighed down by societal pathology and who can appreciate a good glass of merlot and reruns of *Downton Abbey* as much as the next woman. In between heavier mystery fare, this unicorn of a Black cozy is a welcome palate cleanser." —*The Los Angeles Times* on *A Glimmer of Death*

"Fans of cozy mysteries will love this novel about caterer and psychic Dessa Jones." —*Marie Claire* on *A Glimmer of Death*

"Danger, intrigue and adventure ensue in this fun whodunit." —*Woman's World* on *A Fatal Glow*

"Dessa is a complex and relatable adult, not prone to recklessly haring off in order to advance the plot, and an absolute breath of fresh air on the contemporary cozy scene." —*Criminal Element* on *A Fatal Glow*

"The creator of Newark private eye Tamara Hayle dials back the wisecracks and bumps up the paranormal hints to launch a new series featuring a widowed African American Realtor whose workplace is a hot mess." —*Kirkus Reviews* on *A Glimmer of Death*

A
Shimmer
of Red

Valerie Wilson Wesley

Kensington Publishing Corp.
www.kensingtonbooks.com

KENSINGTON BOOKS are published by

Kensington Publishing Corp.
119 West 40th Street
New York, NY 10018

ISBN: 978-1-4967-3966-7 (ebook)

ISBN: 978-1-4967-3965-0

First Kensington Trade Paperback Printing: August 2023

10 9 8 7 6 5 4 3 2 1

Printed in the United States of America

For men who love to read—
Cheo, Booker, Adam, and Robert Pheanious, most of all

Acknowledgments

As always, my sincere gratitude to the many readers and friends who have helped me become a stronger writer. Thank you for continuing to support me. I promise to continue to hone my craft.

My thanks to the Kensington team—Wendy McCurdy, Michelle Addo, Elizabeth Trout, and Larissa Ackerman—for doing far more to help me than I'll ever know.

My love and gratitude to my family—Richard, Thembi, Nandi, and Primo—for their understanding, support, and patience during those days when I truly needed it.

I continue to be grateful to Faith Hampton Childs for her encouragement and simply for being my friend and agent for more years than either of us cares to remember.

I'd also like to give a sincere and belated thank-you to Siobhan Teare, whose advice was essential when I began writing this new series, and thank you, William Jiggetts and Wanda Croudy, for useful information regarding the world of art.

And finally to our family pet Junior, aka Juniper, for making us laugh at the end of the day.

Chapter 1

These were good times in very bad ones. Fear of the pandemic had sent folks scurrying to suburban towns like Grovesville searching for new places to live. Risko Realty, basking in the sun of seller greed and buyer desperation, was selling houses—spacious, modest, tacky, chic—faster than funnel cakes at a Jersey fair. I should have known no good could come of it. If nothing more, the burden of a "gift" I inherited from my mother's people should have forewarned that things would change. But where was that sixth sense that warns that bad times are around the corner or bad folks are headed my way? Nowhere to be found. Even the glimmers weren't glimmering.

Glimmers are the *gift* of my gift that allow me to see what is often called an aura. They are usually a certain color and may vary in shade. A deep reddish purple hints that someone's spirt is in need of healing; a sweet baby pink says tender care should be forthcoming. Glimmers can be intense or hazy depending on how long and hard I stare, which can be awkward, and may change with a person's circumstances or growth. Occasionally they can't be seen or are hard to distinguish, which can be puzzling. Seeing glimmers is among my more predictable extrasensory skills, such as sensing things other people can't. I know that all of this makes me unique, along with the occasional gray streak that can willfully appear on the left side of my head, but often it's a burden. If I'm having trouble understanding any of this, I call my aunt Phoenix, my late mother's older sister, who besides serving up the occasional NJ Pick-4 winner, texts me quotes from Maya Angelou or other bits of wisdom. My aunt is also a source on spells, charms, and the occasional hex. Yet all I received from my aunt during those halcyon days was this puzzling text of Egyptian origin:

A rose can fall to the lot of a monkey.

I wasn't sure if I was the rose or the monkey and didn't care. I was living too high on the hog for it to matter. There was only one sign from the gift I would have heeded during those golden days of selling, and that was the smell of nutmeg. When I smell nutmeg, I know somebody is going to die. The scent can be overpowering or just a whiff, but however it comes, I stop in my tracks, close my eyes, wish that it would go away. Needless to say, I've lost my taste for eggnog, French toast, and bread pudding. But there was no trace of that dreadful spice, and for that I was grateful.

For the first time since my beloved Darryl's sudden death, I was making good money, paying bills on time, even putting money aside for hard times if they ever came back. I bought a dual fuel range oven, new refrigerator, and air fryer, which I didn't need. I upgraded Juniper, my plump little cat, to a pricey cat food blended to help him lose weight, supposedly. I'd even managed to pay back much of the money I owed Aunt Phoenix. I took great pride in that, but as the old saying goes, pride goeth before the fall.

I wasn't the only one riding high at Risko Realty. Tanya

Risko, who had inherited the business thanks to larceny, loathing, and luck, was feeling confident enough to expand "the firm," as she called it, and convinced two young Realtors to leave their companies to join us. They both had made impressive sales, even for these high-selling days, and must not have known about Risko Realty's history, which could kindly be called checkered. Problem was, Tanya was not known for being a wise judge of character. She'd lost two mean-spirited lovers and an abusive husband to foul play in the space of three years yet always landed lightly in her Manolo Blahniks. None of us were sure what to expect when Tanya called us into her office to meet our "new family members."

Yet we had begun to think of ourselves as a family. Our relationship had been tempered by murder and suicide, and healed from trauma as families do—cautiously and fearfully. We were all single and lived alone, except Louella, who had her daughter, Erika, and fiancé, Red. Each of us had endured our own particular bout of sorrow. Me—with the loss of Darryl; Vinton losing Stuart, his lifelong love, to suicide; and Harley coping with his scars from Afghanistan. Despite occasional squabbling, we depended on each other's grace and strength and knew more about each other's weaknesses than we probably should. (Except for the glimmers. Family or not, I wasn't quite ready to share all that!) So we were fearful of disrupting our hard-earned family dynamic when we entered Tanya's office.

Two young women sat stiff and uncomfortable in the cushiony chairs alongside Tanya's desk. Either from respect, discomfort, or nausea from Tanya's honeysuckle candle, they quickly stood when they were introduced.

"Come in, everyone; come right in! I am so pleased to introduce you all to Anna Lee and Bella Mondavi! Anna, show them your pretty smile! Bella Mondavi, lift that head! You are one of the best young Realtors in the county," Tanya said in the overblown style of a mother hen fused with a carnival barker. "Congratulations! You have left your old, tired firm to join our dear, sweet little family!" Tanya was dressed for the occasion in a chic black Chanel suit, a sharp contrast to the bright colors in which she had recently decorated her office; her décor tended to reflect her moods. It had gone from spotlessly white after her husband's murder to girlish paisley prints whenever she fell in love to these vivid shades of orange and yellow. I wondered if the colors were an indication of her glimmer, which I'd glimpsed only once in a vulnerable moment. Tanya Risko was a woman with secrets rarely revealed.

"Welcome to our sweet little family!" said Vinton Laverne, playfully mocking Tanya but playing it off with an innocent smile. "So you both come from the same place?"

"We worked at, uh, Delbarton Estates," said Anna, still smiling and stumbling over the name of her former employer.

"Delbarton Estates? That's the hottest real estate firm in the state!" Vinton whistled long and low emphasizing that point. "Why on earth did you two leave Delbarton?"

"I, uh, had to get out fast. I needed a change," Anna muttered more to herself than to us.

"You're in for a big one here. How about you?" Vincent turned his attention to Bella.

"I needed a change, too. Sometimes you've got to go in a new direction, challenge yourself."

"Well, you're in for a challenge. Hope you don't regret it!" Vinton always said what was on his mind, occasionally revealing more about himself than was wise. It was one of the things I loved about him. He was the oldest among us, quick with quips, which could bite but were less nasty than they'd been when we met. He'd had a sorrowful gray glimmer then, reflected even in the dull, unfashionable suits he wore. But he had changed, wardrobe as well as glimmer. Everything about him these days was younger, trendy, and his glimmer was a pale pleasant blue. "You ladies are coming from some big firms! You two look like schoolgirls. Hard to believe you're old enough to understand a lockbox, say nothing of changing interest rates."

"I'm smarter and older than I look," Anna said, with a hint of attitude that said she was not to be put down. She had a chubby baby face with a receding chin that brought to mind a cute chipmunk until you were drawn to her light brown eyes and flawless chestnut skin. Her hair was chic, short, and bounced coquettishly when she moved her head, which was often. I was struck by her glimmer, a lovely pink shade caught between hot and soft, which made me wonder if she had trouble making up her mind. She was casually dressed with a stylish flare meant to flatter a body that folks of a certain age called pleasingly plump. "I'm just so happy to be here," she added, in a kinder, fluttering voice that reeked sincerity.

"I'll bet you are, smarter than you look. I'm glad you're here, too," said Harley Wilde with a flirtatious touch that brought a raised eyebrow from Vinton. Anna returned a quick engaging smile saying she wasn't offended and was old enough to know it was meant as a compliment, which made Harley drop his eyes slightly in what looked like a blush.

"Well, well, so what do we have here?" said Vinton with a touch of mischief, earning a glance of warning from me. Harley and Anna both ignored him.

Harley Wilde was one of two friends I made when I came to Risko. The other friendship had ended tragically and was still painful to remember. Harley and I shared a mutual love— and craving—for late-morning lattes, which united us from the first, and he never forgot to bring me one when he showed up for work, usually at noon. I'd grown to think of him as the kid brother I always wanted and never had.

I often wondered what Darryl would make of him. Darryl had a special affection for those who had known tough times, like the special needs kids he worked with and the troubled teens he counseled into manhood. He'd understand Harley's vulnerability hidden within that swagger for protection as well as defense, and would take him into his heart, as everyone did who knew him. Harley and I had been through several misadventures that once lived through were rarely discussed again. I knew him well enough to tell when he was scared, happy, or angry, and that he was not shy around women; he'd charmed my two no-nonsense aunts on first meeting. He didn't blush easily.

"I'm glad to be here, too," said Bella Mondavi, unwilling to be left out of the conversation. I could tell she was shy, unsure of herself, which always endears people to me. She was shorter than Anna and petite. Her long blond hair piled in a tight bun and blue eyes gave her a pretty doll-like quality in contrast to her glimmer, which was dark, solemn, and brought to mind the one that had once hung over Vinton. Vinton must have sensed it, too. He reached out for her hand as if to reassure her.

"You're welcomed here, too, sweetheart. You remind me of that little porcelain doll I wanted when I was a kid. You won't break if I give you a hug, will you?" he said, awkwardly reaching out for her.

Stunned, like the rest of us, Bella froze and drew back. But she sized him up in a moment and must have decided he was harmless and not much of a threat. Reluctantly, she gave him a self-conscious hug. I knew that in his own dated way, Vinton was trying to make Bella feel welcomed, but the porcelain doll crack, as sexist as it was racist, was from a different era.

"You've got to forgive Vinton. He just stepped off the *Mad Men* set, a wannabe Don Draper," said Harley, attempting to save the situation.

"Guess I got my decades messed up," Vinton muttered, realizing how he must have sounded. "Best to take my Geritol."

"And now you've added ageism to your sins," I said, peering at him as if he were a naughty child.

"Best to keep my mouth shut," he said after a minute. "Please forgive me."

"Nothing to forgive. I've heard worse. Much worse!" Bella said with the careless shrug of a good sport and an expression that said she had.

"By the way, I'm Dessa," I said, trying to lessen the tension that still filled the room.

"And I'm Harley Wilde," Harley said. "But I'm really not very wild at all." It was an attempt at coyness that ended up being corny and made things worse. Anna gave him a begrudging half smile and a playful roll of her eyes.

Tanya took over from there. "Well, now that everyone knows everybody it's time to get back to work. In our beautiful newly remodeled office space!" she couldn't resist adding. Our tiny cubicles, which we'd managed to get used to, had been separated and spaced in the interest of keeping us healthy. In the interests of saving money, not wasting paint, and making sure nobody dozed off, our cubicles were now the same vibrant colors as her office. "Okay, everybody. We all need to get back to work."

"Ah, the royal *we*," muttered Vinton. Tanya did very little work.

I glanced at Louella, who stood near the back of the room and had said nothing during the introductions. More than anyone else, she'd had a long journey back to normalcy. I suspected she wasn't quite ready to welcome new people into this family she claimed and accepted as her own. I felt a twinge as I caught a glimpse of her old, sad glimmer, which had brought tears whenever I saw her. But it was gone as quickly as it came, and I hoped it would stay gone. The three women were all the same age; Louella was a solitary being in need of a friend her own age. I was more older sister than

confidante, and although Tanya's and Louella's lives inter-
twined in the past, Tanya had made it clear she wasn't interested in maintaining or nurturing female connections.

I caught up with Anna and Bella as we were leaving the
office.

"It's hard being the new person, but believe we all were
once. You two are going to be just fine here," I said as cheerfully as I could. "We're not quite a family, but we're close.
Once you settle in, you'll find we all have a lot in common."
I hoped for Louella's sake that they did. They both nodded,
noncommittally.

"Sparks were sure flying between your boy Harley and the
cute new kid," Vincent said as soon as he could get me alone.
"Let's hope they don't turn into fire. An office romance is
never a good thing. I speak from experience, in case you don't
remember," he said, but of course I did. His love had worked
here, too, and died here as well. "This place does have a way
of taking the life out of you," he added.

A shudder went through me, worrisome because I wasn't
sure what had caused it.

"Everything is going to be fine. Everything is going to be
fine," I said twice, like a robot, reassuring myself.

And everything was fine—for a while. Anna and Bella
became fast friends despite their differences. Anna had a boisterous laugh that drew everybody into it. Bella's cucumber-
cool demeanor forced you to fight for her attention. She grew
up in a once-upon-a-time sundown town in South Jersey that
would never welcome Anna. Anna came of age in a rough-
and-tumble nearby city that would never welcome Bella. But
that didn't matter to either of them. Even with the space between our cubicles, we could hear them talking and laughing
like the schoolgirls Vinton had assumed they were. There was
always some new Mexican or Thai restaurant to discover during lunch or some Netflix series they gossiped about in the

morning. They shared selling tips about properties coming on the market and how best to sell them, and both had that touch that marks the best real estate agents—a mix of compassion, empathy, and serious salesmanship—I sorely lack. They could sell igloos in Costa Rico or thatched huts in Alaska, and racked up more spectacular deals than anybody else at Risko Realty, even outselling Vinton, who had always been the champion. Despite that competitive edginess that marks the real estate business, nobody envied their sales, and we cheered them on with every new win. Except Louella, who seemed to have drifted into herself.

Vinton was right about Harley and Anna, and when she wasn't hanging out with Bella they were heading somewhere together. Although they tried to hide their blossoming relationship from the rest of us, April was a blink away, and for anyone who had ever fallen in love the signs were unmistakable. Their high spirits and simple joy in each other's company was unmistakable, along with the crocuses and daffodils that were popping up everywhere. Springtime was filling a workplace badly in need of ridding itself of the seasonal doom that had darkened its doors.

So when Tanya called me into her office to say that Emily Delbarton, the CEO of Delbarton Estates, wanted me to cater her broker's open house, it seemed just one more good thing heading my way.

A broker's open house is just what it sounds like: an open house opened only for real estate brokers. It's a place for us to assess a property, discuss trends, and generally have a good, professional time with colleagues. You can also count on a great lunch prepared to impress jaded brokers. Delbarton Estates was an influential firm. This was a great opportunity for D&D Delights, the catering company Darryl and I created, to make some important inroads. Brokers from around the state would be there, and in the future would be serving refreshments at their own open houses, both to clients as well as to other brokers. Having my business cards handily tucked away in that many wallets was an opportunity not to be missed.

"It's a real compliment to Risko Realty that she wants you to do it; out of all the caterers in the world, she thought of Risko Realty!" said Tanya, missing the point entirely. "Just make sure you do a good job. We don't want any more Casey Osbornes hanging over our heads."

"I'm not the one who hung Casey Osborne over our heads!" I said more harshly than I meant to. I wasn't about to let Tanya hang *that* one on me.

"Well, you know what I mean," she said, sheepishly. "I just don't want, well, you know, any more trouble like what happened before. Things are going so good. You know what I mean, Dessa; I just don't want any more trouble." The little-girl voice she pulled out when she needed it softened my attitude to gain my sympathy as it always did.

"Don't worry," I said, managing a smile. But then again, how could I be sure? The memory of Casey Osborne lying cold as a dead trout at my feet still haunted me.

"Emily Delbarton said she got your name from her brother Edgar. Do you remember catering anything for him? Well, it doesn't matter. At least they know who we are. But it's only two weeks from now! Will you have enough time to do a good job?" she said in a worried rush of words. The fate of Risko Realty, after all, was in my hands.

"Sure. No big thing!" I said confidently. These days nothing seemed beyond my reach. "We'll be planning and cooking, not serving, and I'll get Louella to help me out." If nothing more, this was also a good chance for me to reach out to Louella, whose sales had dipped precariously. "There are just too many of us here," she'd said more than once, always with a glance at Anna and Bella.

That dark glimmer that had shrouded her spirit the first

time I saw her was back, coming and going more since their arrival. I knew she was threatened by their success, and probably jealous of them. She had been the youngest member of our family, the "baby" in a certain way, and like a displaced child she now had to share that cherished spot with cuter siblings. At least once a day, she threatened to quit. I begged her to wait, promising that things would get better. It was the same thing her mother had often told me in my first terrible days, and they did. I was glad to be able to share those words with her. Helping me cater an event would be a way for her to focus on something else. Cooking is therapeutic. Between the planning, measuring, stirring, baking, and finally tasting, it's always healed me. Maybe it would do the same for Louella. We had time to shop, and it wouldn't take long to prep and cook.

A few days before the event, Emily Delbarton had the house opened so Louella and I could see the kitchen and the dining room where the food would be served. When we walked into the place, both of us caught our breath. It had been a loser of a Victorian that had been on the market for two years, and even the best Realtors had never gotten a bite. But gone was the tacky wallpaper, rickety furniture, and disgusting moldy smell that seemed to seep in from everywhere. If money had a smell, this place had its scent, and somebody had gone hog wild in the showrooms of the New York Design Center. Everything, from rugs to light fixtures, was contemporarily chic. Elegant white walls now displayed stunning works of art that transformed each room. Delbarton Estates, known for turning duds into diamonds, had clearly worked their magic, making this dreary property into a dream house.

A young woman standing on a step stool in the living room was carefully positioning an abstract oil painting over the fireplace. "Done," she said, gracefully stepping off the stool. She turned to face us, her darting eyes deciding whether we were worthy of her time. "Hi, I'm Rosalie Davis," she finally said, extending a hand, far too young for the antique emerald ring she wore. "Emily and I are trying to get this place ready to show in two days. It's almost there."

"This is your house?" asked Louella like a wonderstruck child; the question had occurred to me, too.

Rosalie's laugh was soft yet dismissive. The two women were roughly the same height, but Rosalie managed to lift her head just high enough so that she peered down. "No, of course not," she said as if amused.

"Sorry," Louella stuttered, obviously embarrassed.

"I recognize that work. It's a Romare Bearden collage," I said, pointing toward the abstract painting she was hanging. "Obviously, it's not the real thing."

She turned to me, surprised. "Obviously not. It's a photograph of a rare one. How did you know what it was?"

"Another life," I said, turning away from the prying eyes trying to figure me out. Her smile that wasn't one came too quickly, and didn't expect to be returned. I looked hard for a glimmer and finally caught a puzzling one that shifted colors too quickly for me to distinguish, a rare occurrence.

Rosalie Davis had the kind of willowy good looks that rich ladies' clothes are designed for. Her flawless cashew-colored skin along with her classically oval face begged to be photographed and her arrogant bearing and perfect teeth hinted that she'd grown up with money and the self-confidence that it brings, which explained the emerald ring.

"You two must be here to cook for the open house?"

"We're catering it, yes," I said neutrally. "But we're also Realtors with Risko Realty." I hoped she'd never heard of the place, because of its questionable reputation.

"You must work with Anna Lee," she said, suddenly interested.

"Yeah, we do."

"Tell her I said hello, and that I'm looking forward to see-ing her again."

"Sure," I said, surprised by her curiosity.

"This house is incredible!" said Louella, her eyes grow-ing big.

"Yes, it is," said Rosalie. "Well, I'm going to let you two do whatever you came here to do, and be on my way," she said, then added as an afterthought, "You might be interested in these." She opened a stylish leather pack and pulled out two pale silver business cards with *Reset by Rosalie* printed across them in fancy embossed script.

"Reset?" Louella, obviously in awe, said after reading the card.

"If you're selling a property, call me if you need to stage it. *Staging* means—"

"We know what *staging* means. And you're right; we'd better do what we came here to do," I said, politely dismis-sive.

I don't like being rude to people. It's bad for the soul, as Aunt Phoenix, who is routinely rude to people, reminds me. But Louella was more vulnerable than she'd been in two years, and Rosalie's condescension plucked a nerve.

"Give me a call, I will help you sell a house," she said, ig-noring me and speaking directly to Louella, who was clutch-ing the card like the Holy Grail. "And we can work out some kind of deal after the house is sold, and it will be sold," she added with a wink as she walked away.

"Did you hear that! Rosalie must be a genius. Her staging has really turned this house around!" Louella said as soon as she was out of sight.

"Along with Delbarton money. But she's probably good at what she does," I said begrudgingly.

"Why do you think Anna Lee *really* left Delbarton Es-tates?" Louella asked after a moment.

"I think it's just like Anna said; she just got tired of it." But as I looked around the room, I was beginning to wonder myself.

"I don't believe her. I don't know about Bella, but that girl, Anna, is not all she seems to be. She may have fooled Harley and the rest of you all, but she hasn't fooled me!"

"Oh, give the girl a break!" I said, losing patience. "You've had an attitude ever since she and Bella came. What's going on?" I turned toward her, forcing her to face me.

Snatching herself away, Louella shrugged, clearly unwilling to share her feelings.

"Sometimes, you've got to be the one to reach out to people. Take that extra step. Be friendly to them first!"

"I've stepped as far as I'm going to step. I'll be friendly when they're friendly to me," she snapped back. "But I'm definitely going to give Rosalie Davis a call. I know she'll help me change my luck. So what are our plans for this open house?" she said, eager to change the subject.

"We'll plan on Saturday. It will be fun," I said, hoping that it would.

That weekend Louella, with Erika and Red in tow, came over for an easy dinner of roasted chicken, baked potatoes, and honeyed carrots. While Red and Erika cleaned up afterwards (Erika sneaking greedy Juniper bits of leftovers that he begged for), Louella and I settled down in my office to plan our event. We worked well together, and her mood and confidence seemed to grow the longer we talked. Now wasn't the time, I decided, to ask her what was going on about Anna and Bella or scold her about her attitude.

We decided on platters of cheese and fancy crackers and crudités along with a selection of finger foods: pinwheels filled with various spreads, smoked salmon bites on crostini, caprese skewers, bruschetta, and the old dependable pigs in a blanket. A dessert table with cookies and chocolate-covered cherries and truffles would be nearby, as well as one for beverages. We ordered the crudités and dessert and cheese platters from a pricey gourmet place to be delivered to the house the morning of the event. The finger foods were easy and quick enough to prepare the day before or early that morning.

"Let's hope nobody drops dead," said Louella, half joking and echoing a fear I refused to acknowledge.

"Don't be silly!" I snapped, uttering a silent prayer to the catering gods who protect good cooks from bad clams and milk gone sour.

And everything was perfect that day, and nobody dropped dead. That came later, in a violent murder that left us all reeling with grief. It was only then I admitted to myself I'd caught a whiff of nutmeg that afternoon and ignored it just as I had those frightening glimmers I pretended not to see.

Chapter 2

The Risko Realty crew showed up together. Just like family. Tanya led the way, dismissing the drop-dead gorgeous house with a cool, to-the-manor-born nod. Nobody else was so nonchalant. Folks oohed and aahed all the way to the refreshment tables where Louella and I were patiently waiting.

"Oh my God, Sweetie, ever seen a place like this?" said Vinton to Bella, piling his luncheon plate full of pigs in a blanket and smoked salmon.

"Leave some room for dessert," Bella cautioned. "Don't forget that diet you said you were on."

"Another day, Sweetie, another day!" he said, grabbing some cheese and chocolate chip cookies from the dessert table. After their initial awkward introduction, Bella and Vinton had become good friends, and he'd even given her a nickname, which was only bestowed on certain people: mine was Sunshine, Louella's Baby Doll. I wondered if his sudden closeness to Bella was another reason Louella disliked the two women, though as far as I knew it was only Bella who had received that particular blessing. "Have you ever seen anything like this in your life?" Vinton continued, his eyes darting this

way and that like those of a kid walking into a traveling carnival.

"All I can say is, wow!" Harley said, heaping his plate full
of sandwiches and chocolate cherries as he joined the conversation.

"Wow the house or wow the spread?" I couldn't resist
asking.

"Both, of course!" Anna, who stood beside him, playfully
scolded. I chuckled to myself; they were already acting like a
married couple.

"Thank you, baby, always saving my behind!" Harley gave
her a quick kiss on the forehead, and moved a chocolate cherry
from the serving plate to hers. "I'll eat enough for both of us,
corny but true," he said.

She shook her head vigorously and gave it back. "Thanks,"
she said with a self-conscious grin. "You're always looking
out for me."

"Always, never doubt that," he said, but Anna's attention
had gone to someone else.

"Emily Delbarton really did it up this time," she said, her
voice low.

"Her and Rosalie Davis," added Harley.

"Yeah, Rosalie. She definitely makes her presence known."

"Did somebody say my name?" asked Rosalie in a charming, modest voice as she closed in on Harley and Anna. She
reached for a cracker from the cheese platter and added it
along with the two baby carrots on her nearly empty plate.
"It's good to see you again, Anna. Always great to see you."

Anna forced a shy, weak smile. "Nice to see you, too.
You know I don't work for Emily anymore, right?"

"I heard, and who are you?" She turned to give Harley a
quick, appraising once-over. "You're a Realtor, too?"

"No, I'm just here with my lady," he said, which changed

Anna's half smile into a full, beaming one. "We work together at Risko Realty," he added, trying to cover Anna's puzzling discomfort.

"So you must work with them, too, right? The caterers?" Rosalie nodded toward me and Louella still standing near the refreshment table. "Here are my cards; please take some. I staged this house for Emily. This is *all* my work!" Taking a nibble off a carrot, she'd leapt from modest to haughty in the space of a breath.

"Staged the mess out of it, too, as far as I can tell," agreed Vinton, moving closer to the group. "Give me one of those cards. No! I'll take two," he added, taking three.

Everyone chuckled at his enthusiasm, except Anna. Something had grabbed her attention, and my gaze followed hers.

Emily Delbarton moved across the crowded room with the poise and self-assurance that tall women possess and old money guarantees. Delbarton Estates, begun by her great-grandfather when Jersey land was cheap, had been a fixture in real estate for generations. The family had other money-making ventures these days, but selling and buying properties was the source of their wealth and although less profitable than it had been was what they were known for. She was a striking woman, if not a pretty one. Her long face, wrinkled and tan, spoke of too much fun in the sun, and her short blond hair bleached a striking platinum underscored it. No Chanel suits, diamond earrings, or heels worth a working woman's wages for Emily Delbarton; she was beyond all that.

It was clear to anyone who looked hard that wealth was something she took for granted, like others might a warm bed or bacon with breakfast. Yet there was something else about her that struck me. Her glimmer was an odd shade of bronze, not quite gold nor copper but one I'd never seen before. Maybe money had something to do with it; rich folks crossed my path as often as five bucks on a sidewalk. Her glimmer made me uncomfortable; I wasn't sure why. Intuitively I drew away. That was one thing the "gift" was good for, sharpening instincts—a wariness of things unknown, like a cautious kid feels before petting a runaway dog. Not everyone was so cautious. Tanya hurried to greet the woman with such unbridled enthusiasm I feared she would curtsy.

"I can't tell you what a pleasure it is to finally meet you," she said, her voice breathless, words tumbling from her mouth. "I'm the CEO of Risko Realty. You have always been such an inspiration to me, ever since I was a girl."

I managed to keep a straight face. Vinton, not so successful, pulled his into an ill-timed grimace. "Has she forgotten Charlie? Who the heck does she think she's fooling?" he stage-whispered in my ear. I shook my head in dismay. I could understand his impatience with Tanya Risko, but there were things about her past she had shared with me that earned her a soft spot in my heart. We both knew, however, that our Tanya was and had been many things in her short, sweet life and an Emily Delbarton clone was not one of them.

If the woman guessed that Tanya was only imagining a life unlived, she didn't let on. Delbarton graciously extended her hand, which Tanya grabbed, noting, I was sure, the three-carat solitaire diamond that glistened on her ring finger, the one and only piece of jewelry she wore. "Thank you so much. I've heard such interesting things about Risko Realty," she said without a hint of sarcasm. Everyone in earshot visibly cringed. "As a matter of fact, I recently lost one of my . . . my agents to your firm," she added, anxiously glancing around. "She was here a minute ago; where did she go?"

"You must be talking about Anna Lee. She had nothing but praise for you and Delbarton Estates, and I'd like to add, you have done wonders with this house!" Tanya added, clearly eager to change the subject. We all knew Anna had said nothing about Delbarton Estates except she was glad to be out of there.

"Yes," Emily Delbarton muttered, as if she hadn't heard her. She had turned away, as if searching the room. I wondered if she was looking for Anna, and why her whereabouts were suddenly so important. I began to look, too, curious as to where she had gone, especially without Harley, who stood where he'd been. He began searching, too, as if just realizing she wasn't beside him.

The room was packed with Realtors by then, schmoozing, gossiping, eating, laughing, wondering how big a commission this Delbarton place would bring. I was pleased to see how quickly the food was gobbled up and how generously the compliments were flowing. Our stack of business cards on the dessert table was disappearing, too, but not nearly as fast as those of Rosalie Davis, which she had placed on a small silver platter next to ours.

"We should have put our cards in something fancy. That girl is so smart!" said Louella, her voice brimming with admiration. "I can't wait to work with her. I know my luck will change!"

"Well, if she takes one of your old houses and fixes it up like this, you're probably right," I said, but was doubtful. Most of Louella's clients wouldn't be in the market for a house like this one, staged or not. "We'll do something cute next time," I said with a reassuring pat. "Maybe put Erika in a little apron and chef's hat and she can hand them out. That cute enough?" The thought of Erika doing something special made us both chuckle, and from the looks of things I was sure there would be a next time.

"I just hope Rosalie remembers what she promised about giving me a break when it came to money. I don't have enough to pay for a reset. I'm not Delbarton Estates. Do you think she'll remember?" Concern dimmed the smile that had brightened her face.

"If she said she'd give you a break I'm sure she will." Although the more I watched Rosalie Davis in action, the less convinced I was. She briefly chatted with Louella at the beginning of the event but hadn't spoken to her since. But she stayed close to Bella and Anna, talking and tittering as if they'd known each other before. When she wasn't with them, she was circling the room, grinning, handing out cards, but never far from Emily Delbarton, answering questions with her pleasant smile.

I couldn't blame her for promoting her "brand." Things were going good for me, too. Several agents with pending open houses made me promise I'd cater theirs. To my surprise, Emily Delbarton tore herself away from her admirers to ask if I'd do more catering for her.

"Perhaps, you can drop by with sample menus within the next few days. Give me a call and we'll set up a time."

I could hardly believe my luck. "Thank you so much; I'd love that," I said, barely hiding my excitement. Despite the woman's questionable glimmer, I wasn't about to let my dubious familial gift get in the way of making a buck.

"Do you know where Anna Lee went?" Her abrupt question took me by surprise.

"I'm sorry, I don't." She turned to look at something across the room, drawing my gaze as well.

Although the two men entered at the same time, they weren't together and neither looked like he belonged. The taller one seemed to be desperately searching for somebody. He had a heavyweight's body and a cock-of-the-walk belligerence, which along with sunglasses and dreadlocks in a sumo-wrestling knot said, *Do not mess with me.* I looked hard for a glimmer and saw a hint of one that didn't make sense. It was a pale pinkish tint that came and went so quickly I assumed my eyes were playing tricks. Another glimmering puzzler to take up with the resident glimmer expert.

The glimmer of the shorter one was as startling as his hair, which was slick and so black it had to be dyed. It contrasted sharply with his pale skin nearly the color of his white linen suit. But the glimmer was what got me. It had a green cast to it, the color of pistachio nuts. According to Aunt Phoenix, green typically meant envy, which made me think of Georgia, the young woman who worked the counter in Lennox Royal's restaurant. I wondered who here had inspired such a color. Where had they come from? I turned to ask Harley, but he had disappeared. Vinton, who was closing in on what was left of the chocolate chip cookies, eagerly shared his thoughts.

"What corner of hell did those two step out of?"

"You don't know them either?"

"Heck no! What do you take me for, Sunshine? I stopped hanging out with weirdos like that when I left my twenties, long before I hooked up with Stu. The big one looks like somebody's bodyguard, but this isn't that kind of crowd. The skinny one?" He shrugged. "Vampire? Horror movie?"

"I think I've seen one of them before," said Bella, sounding worried and perplexed. "But I don't remember when or where."

"Nightmare, maybe? Stay away from them, Sweetie."

She shook her head, as if something was bothering her. "Where's Anna?" she said, sounding alarmed.

"Look for Harley," said Vinton. "They're probably on that tour of the house, which is where I'm heading now." He put his empty plate on the table and hurried off in the direction of a small group of Realtors who were heading up the stairs.

"Maybe I should go, too," said Bella.

"Rosalie said she'd take me on a private tour after everybody was gone." Louella joined us with a hint of smugness. "Rosalie says she can tell me some of the finer points that can help me sell. Wouldn't it be something if I could actually make a sale on this place! A sale like that would fix me for life," she said, her voice and eyes turning dreamy.

"Not quite," I said, hating to dim her hopes for the big time. "But it would definitely get your picture in the *Real Estate Times*."

"That's such a nice gesture! Can me and Anna tag along?" Bella asked, and Louella's face dropped.

"Well, I don't know she only promised me," she said, hesitating, like a possessive third grader holding on to a new doll.

"I'll ask her. Harley's talking to her now. Maybe he can come, too." Bella moved toward Harley and Rosalie, just as he was leaving and heading to me.

"She's not in the house. Rosalie said she saw her rush out. She said 'rush,' not run! Why do you think she left like that? What's going on?" His voice was louder than it should have been and filled with dread.

"Did you try calling her?"

"It went to voicemail."

"Probably went to get something out of her car."

"We drove over here together. Something is wrong! I know it. I'm going to go outside and see if she's okay."

Anna stepped back into the house then, and even from where we stood I could see she was crying. Harley rushed over to her, tried to hug her but she pulled away, apparently unwilling to share what had upset her. Bella, realizing what was going on, went to join the two of them with Rosalie close behind her. They sat Anna down on the white couch, where none of the Realtors had dared to sit, and the two women hovered over her like protective, loving sisters. After a while, Rosalie went into the kitchen and brought back a glass of water. Harley, crestfallen, watched in silence.

"Woman business, I guess," he finally said, sounding dejected.

"She didn't tell you what happened?"

"No!"

"She'll tell you later," I said, trying to reassure him, "Truth is even the closest of couples don't tell each other everything about themselves. You got to leave some mystery to keep the magic alive," I said, but didn't believe it. Darryl and I had shared so much about ourselves I knew the finer points of his history better than my own. "If it's important she'll say what has upset her when she feels comfortable doing it. Let her have some time."

Reluctantly, he nodded in agreement. "You know more about women and relationships than me, I guess. But, well, I've never seen her this upset."

"She probably wants to run things by Bella, get her advice before she tells you. Don't worry, sooner or later you'll know. If it's really important, she'll tell you." He looked relieved and nodded as if he knew I was right, and I hoped that I was.

Yet it must have been far more serious than I thought. She didn't tell him later that day, that night, or even weeks after that, when nothing could be said.

When the open house ended, Harley helped me haul my dishes and supplies back to my car. When he came back inside to look for Anna, he found that she and Bella had already gone. Louella, sulking and angry, sat by herself in a dark corner of the dated, ugly kitchen, the only part of the house left untouched by Reset Rosalie.

"Anna's gone. The three of them squeezed into Rosalie's ritzy old-fashioned car and drove away. Probably went out for dinner or drinks or whatever cute little rich girls do," Louella said when Harley asked.

"What are you talking about?" Harley snapped, clearly annoyed. "Nobody's rich, so they all left together; maybe they were still talking! Why would you say something mean like that?"

Louella shrugged and didn't answer; the old glimmer, the one that had marked her the first time we met, had settled around her. "Maybe they found out about what happened in my past. About what I've done. Who I am and . . ." She didn't finish the sentence. She didn't need to. Harley and I both knew what she was talking about. Her words brought back our collective memories of those heartbreaking days. I assumed that was why that whiff of nutmeg I suddenly smelled seemed to come from nowhere.

"Anna's not like that. She doesn't hold stuff from people's past against them," Harley continued, clearly angry.

"They didn't even bother to say good-bye," Louella said, more to herself than to us. "Nobody. Not Anna, Bella, or even Rosalie Davis, and she promised she'd show me the house when everybody was gone. It was like I was nothing, like I didn't exist." It was the tremor in her voice that touched me. Harley heard it, too, but wasn't sure how to react or what comfort to offer her.

"Just forget about it!" he snapped. "You take things too serious sometimes. Not everybody is out to get you or hold your past against you." Louella, saying nothing, just stared at him hard. Her glimmer was back, and that worried me.

Days later when the TV news reported that a young woman's body had been found on the side of the road, I couldn't stop trembling. I kept calling Louella, desperately letting the phone ring until she answered. Only then was I able to breathe again, drink chamomile tea, fall off to sleep. But early that next morning, Harley was at my front door, banging and crying as he tried to wake the dead.

Chapter 3

Sometimes all you can do is hug somebody, pull him close, offer a piece of your heart. We stood there, me holding Harley like he was a kid, neither of us speaking because neither of us could. I knew what had happened. The gift had no say in the matter, just the sorrow etched in his face. It was Monday morning, but there was no going to work. I brought him into the house, settled him down in the middle of the couch forgetting it was the favorite spot of Juniper, who to his credit jumped out of the way, then cuddled up to Harley like he'd known him all his life. Juniper always knew when I was upset, nestling when I needed warm comfort, licking my hand with his rough little tongue. He snuggled up to Harley now, gazing up and purring softly as if he wanted to make things better. Harley glanced down at him and then away, too filled with anguish to acknowledge anything but pain. I let him sit silently for a while. He needed time as much as I did.

"Can you tell me what happened?" I said.

He took a long, then short, quick breath. "I should have gone with her," he said, his voice hoarse and cracking. "If I'd done that she wouldn't be dead. I should have made her tell me where she was going, followed her even, to keep her safe."

"Anna?" I asked, although I knew. Who else could it be? "Where should you have gone?"

He slumped down, wept some more, made himself stop. "I can't quit crying, Dessa. I'm acting like some kind of a stupid baby or something. I'm a grown man, for God's sake. Been through a war, fights and stuff I can't talk about that should have taken me out. I should have more control over myself than this. But I just can't stop!"

I nodded because I understood. "Just let it take you over." I'd done my share of crying but didn't tell him what I knew about grief and how it would change you in ways you couldn't know. He'd find that out himself, and there would be time for that if he asked. But I needed to know more now. I asked again as gently as I could, "Where should you have gone?"

"With her last night. I'd told her so many times not to run alone at night, but she was always watching her weight and stuff, careful about what she ate, only eating certain foods, and exercising, always running. Didn't she know she was perfect the way she was? She didn't get it, and she didn't listen. Why did she go there? Why didn't she believe me when I told her?" His words poured out in a ragged stream of sorrow and disbelief, and I knew those questions would haunt him forever. Then he smiled slightly as if recalling some endearing thing about her, and I thought about those moments of remembered joy that would come and leave within a heartbeat after I lost Darryl.

I knew now who the woman was who had been found on the side of the road. I'd been so grateful and relieved it wasn't Louella that it hadn't occurred to me that another young woman had been brutally killed. The reality of Anna Lee's death slowly began to seep in, shaking me to my core. Harley stared straight ahead as if through will alone he could gain control. "I'm going to put on some water for tea, and I'll bring you a cup when it's ready," I said, unsure he heard me until he looked up, his eyes blank. He shook his head slightly as if dislodging some terrible thought.

I needed to clear my own head, so I stepped outside onto my porch. The *Star-Ledger* lay on the sidewalk in front of the house and I picked it up, hoping to find out more about the accident. Not yet ready to go back inside, I sat down on my top stair trying to calm the feelings that flooded through me. I breathed in the morning air, held it, then let it go, pushing out the sadness. Harley's questions were now my own.

It was a typical Monday morning on my block, kids heading to the corner for the bus, laden down with backpacks too heavy for their small shoulders, parents, lingering in their doorways watching them go before heading to work or the train. I took in the everyday peace of this small world, grateful for the corner where I'd lived the happiest days of my life, and finally, after these last few years, knowing I might still be happy again.

Slowly and surely, this place was changing. One of the boys who lived next door was off to Morehouse College, and the other was headed to his junior year in high school. All that remained was the occasional bounce of a backyard basketball in what had once seemed their never-ending game. They were becoming men before my eyes, which made me happy for their hardworking mother and sad that Darryl hadn't been around long enough to see them grow up. Good can come when you least expect it, same as bad. Life has a way of changing when you dared take it for granted. It had been for me and now was for Harley. Nothing stays the same. Ever.

"Out here enjoying this beautiful morning; gorgeous, isn't it?" said my neighbor Julie Russell, snatching me from my thoughts. "I heard the roar of a motorcycle out here a while ago, then someone banging like crazy on your door. Every-thing okay inside?" she added in her unique blend of cheer and nosiness.

I smiled to myself. That was one thing that hadn't changed: Julie's inquisitiveness. But she meant well. Women living alone need to look out for each other, she constantly reminded me. I appreciated her looking out for me. Although she was a small woman and older than me by decades, I suspected with wit and will alone she could tackle any evildoer who dared sneak on to our porches meaning either of us harm.

"Just a friend from work," I said.

"Trouble?"

"Needed to talk, that's all."

"Did you hear about the girl that was hit on that road near the park? What a tragedy!"

"Yes, it was," I said.

With her abiding love of newspapers and the local TV news, sooner or later she'd find out whatever she wanted to know without me saying anything. I also knew she'd be eager to talk about it, and I wasn't ready to talk.

"Well, I'm glad to know all is okay. But the roar of that bike got my attention. Don't hear too many motorcycles around here at this time of the morning. Any time of the morning!"

I nodded in agreement, giving my friend that, then added as a second thought, "Thanks for looking out for me, Julie. I appreciate it."

She smiled shyly. "I'm glad you do. I don't hear from my daughter as often as I'd like to. I get on her nerves with all my questions. Well, at least I can talk to you, and I'm happy for that. Hope I don't annoy you, too," she added with concern. She stepped back with the *Star-Ledger* and the *New York Times* clutched in each hand, not giving me the chance to answer.

I opened the newspaper, anxiously searching the opening

pages for something about Anna, but found nothing. I tore through the rest of the pages with the bitter knowledge that if she had been a young white woman it would have been front-page news. Finally, right before the obits and advertisements, I found the headline:

Woman Found Dead Hit-and-Run Suspected

It was disrespectful, an insult to the memory of Anna, even though it simply stated the facts as known. I buried my anger and forced myself to finish reading.

> *Anna Lee, 23, a Grovesville resident, was identified on Sunday morning as the victim of vehicular homicide on Parksmith Drive, an isolated stretch of road frequented by joggers. Police state her death probably occurred late Saturday night.*

The article went on to state that she was a Realtor at Risko Realty, a local Grovesville real estate agency, and that the police were in the process of contacting next of kin. It also said that although vehicular homicides were difficult to solve, the Grovesville police department would continue to investigate it as they did other major crimes. I rolled my eyes in disgust. As I had firsthand knowledge of the investigative skills of the local police force, that was like hoping for sun in the middle of a snowstorm. Those guys knew as much about solving a crime as I did about loading a shotgun. There was no solace for me and certainly none for Harley, but at least I knew some details.

I stuffed the newspaper deep into my recycling bin in the kitchen, then boiled water for tea, nothing herbal or fancy, just something that went well with honey and milk. I toasted some white bread and buttered it generously. It was food plucked from the sick days of childhood, and the memory of my mother watching me nibble warm buttered toast and sip hot ginger tea laced with honey and lemon like I'd seen her and Aunt Phoenix do. My aunt, with whom we lived during those days, was dismissive of my mother's tender remedies. Her suggestion for whatever ailed you was a nasty brew concocted from echinacea roots—unsweetened, pungent, unappetizing. Wood tea was what I called it, and balked at its supposedly curative abilities. I knew even then that it was the presence of my mother that really did the curing, warm and caring beside me, and for the first time this day I smiled at the memory. I put the buttered toast on a saucer, poured hot water with teabags into a blue ceramic teapot, and loaded everything, along with honey and a small pitcher of milk, onto a tray, carrying it into the living room and placing it on the maple coffee table in front of the sofa.

As the tea steeped, I reflected on the number of souls who had found comfort in this pale pink room sitting on this aging gray couch. When Darryl and I bought it all those years ago, little did we know what role it would play in the healing of people's lives. It was cheap, soft, and in good shape, a grand find for bargain hunters, and nearly matched the two easy chairs we'd bought the month before. We grinned and celebrated our lucky day all the way home. The sun that managed to cut through the gloom of that lingering day of winter in March, and our smug excitement about our good deal made everything all the better.

So much had been lost since then. I made myself focus on what had come since. This room, still infused with our love, had brought more comfort to others than we could ever have imagined. Tanya Risko, a woman not known for tact or thoughtfulness, found solace here after the death of her cheating lover. Lacey, a teenager who was still part of my life, had fallen asleep on this couch after a frightening day turned into night. Was it the yielding nature, giving itself over to whomever settled into it? More likely, it was Darryl's spirit that lived here with me, that only I and Juniper could see. I smiled again, for the second time this morning; the thought of him always lightened whatever mood I was in.

Harley, suddenly aware I was there, glanced up, then poured a cup of tea, adding more honey than he probably needed.

"You remembered! Thanks, Dessa. Sipping it reminds me of her, my mom."

"I do remember." He'd told me how his mother brewed tea in a pot, never in a cup, and that the gesture brought her back to him whenever he made tea. That had been a terrible day, but everything had ended up fine. This one never would.

I knew Harley's mother only through his memories and the goodwill of her friends in the Aging Readers Club who looked out for him when he needed rescuing. There was no rescuing him now, nothing Laura Grace or her kindred spirits could say or do to soften this wounding blow. Sooner or later in his own time and way, he would tell them about Anna and what he had lost. He'd reached out to me this morning because he knew the grief I'd lived through and I knew Anna and would share his devastating loss.

Harley finished up his tea and poured another cup. "What kind is it? Doesn't taste like Lipton's."

"Earl Grey. Reminds me of Darryl." Except Darryl was the quintessential Trekkie, liked his Earl Grey with milk, like Picard.

He nibbled at the toast, slowly savoring each bite.

We sat there quietly while he finished, then spoke hesitantly, as if unsure about what to say. "Hey, Dess, I need to ask you something." His tone, wary and cautious, reminding me of his voice that night on the phone telling me he was in jail and asking my help. I tried to hide my momentary discomfort, but he knew me too well for that. "At least, I'm not in the slammer this time," he said with a half smile. A good sign, a reminder that Harley was still there, underneath all his grief.

"Just say it. Don't worry about it. I can't read your mind," I said, as if taking him lightly. He avoided my eyes, still unsure. "It can't be that bad." I managed a tight smile that ended up looking like a grimace.

"It's kind of like, well, intrusive."

"Intrusive? What? You want to move in here with Parker?" The mention of his pet parakeet brought a fleeting shimmer of light into his eyes.

"Anna liked Parker. Not everybody would put up with a parakeet like him."

You got that right, I thought but didn't say.

"He's good company," he added after a minute.

"Animals always are. What kind of intrusion are you talking about?" I said, eager to get back to the subject at hand.

"I keep thinking that if me and Anna had had this app called Life360 on our phones, like if we'd had that, I would have known where she was, I would have been there for her, I would have . . ." He paused again, waiting for my reaction. "Well, you're like family to me, Dessa. I don't have a lot of people I'm close to. I feel sometimes like we're blood kin, even though I know we're not. And I was wondering. . . ."

"You want me to download some app on my phone? Exactly what does it do?" I said, dismayed and surprised at the same time.

"It shows you where people are, tells you their location. It can help you track somebody if you're worried about them."

"Harley, we're close friends but . . ."

"I can't lose anybody else. I lost my mom, now Anna. . . . What if you're in trouble and need my help, what . . ." He stumbled over the words, then stopped and shrugged. "It was a dumb thing to ask. I'm sorry, Dess. You don't want me in

your business any more than I want you in mine," he added
with a sigh he didn't bother to hide.

"And this would make you feel better if I have this track-
ing app on my iPhone? I may not have much of a social life
now, but I don't want somebody to know where I am every
minute of the day."

"You're right! I'm sorry I asked, Dess; it's just . . ."

He looked so crestfallen I had to say something. "Maybe
we can try it for a month and see how it works. I don't expect
to be in any trouble or be anywhere . . . I want to keep secret.
Not at this point anyway. Would that make you feel better?"
I said, softening my voice.

"If I don't hear from you in a couple of days then I can
look out for you?"

"A couple of days, not every hour or something," I said,
not entirely convinced.

"Only if I think you need my help."

"Which I won't. It is not going to happen, but you can
look for me if you are worried. You'll have to show me how
to hook it up. What's the other thing you want to ask me
about?" I was almost scared to ask.

"Can you go over there with me, to where it happened? I
need to put some flowers down, something she liked. Put
them where . . ."

He couldn't finish the sentence and I didn't make him.

"Why don't you go buy the flowers you need, and we'll
drive over there this afternoon."

After another cup of tea and two pieces of toast, I sent
Harley on his way. The moment he closed the door, Aunt
Phoenix sent a text, as she is prone to do when she "knows"
I'm distressed.

**However long the night may last, there will be
morning—a Moroccan proverb.**

I called her back because I needed to hear the reassurance of her voice. "At least I know what this one means," I said.

"Are you talking about the monkey and the rose? That's not clear to you yet? Wait around, darling; it will be," she said with a chuckle.

"I didn't know what to say to him," I said, assuming as I always did with my aunt that she knew what was on my mind without an explanation.

"You said what you needed to say."

"Do you or Aunt Celestine know any . . ."

"Don't be foolish," she said sternly. "There's no spell or potion or anything else that can cure heartbreak. If we knew one, we would have given it to you. Just be careful when you go over there with him tonight."

"Tonight? We're going as soon as he gets back."

But my aunt was right, of course. It took Harley most of the day to collect a bouquet that he felt was lovely and worthy enough to celebrate Anna, and when we finally found the place where she died it was night and close to the time that she had been killed.

Chapter 4

The chill came, lingered, disappeared like a shudder. The area was surrounded by yellow police tape that had been trampled into the ground, so I knew that this was where Anna had died. A straggly bunch of flowers had been tossed haphazardly on the ground directly inside the tape. It was an uninspiring bouquet—two-day-old tulips, wilting daisies bunched and held together by a red rubber band, most likely bought on the spur of the moment at an Acme or ShopRite. Yet someone had taken the time to place them here, boldly crossing the police tape to do so. As we pulled up, a black Ford pickup truck pulled away, making a wide U-turn and nearly hitting us. The road was dangerously narrow and dark, just like it must have been when Anna was killed. The windshield was tinted, so I couldn't tell who was driving, and I assumed whoever it was had left the flowers. Harley, clutching his huge bouquet in his arms, didn't see the truck, and I was grateful for that. But he frowned when he saw the dying bouquet.

"Who do you think left these?" he said in bewilderment, more to himself than me. I had a sense who did but wasn't about to tell him. "You think it could have been somebody from work? Maybe Louella or Vinton? Did you tell them what happened?"

"No, but I think everybody knows it by now. It was on TV last night and in the newspaper this morning. Whoever it was cared about Anna; that's all that matters."

"Do you think this is where it happened?"

"This is a good place to leave the flowers," I said, not addressing his question. He stepped over the tape and carefully placed his bouquet on the ground. Besides the tape, there was no visible sign as to where it had happened. No upturned ground or mown-down weeds. Harley's bouquet was glorious—a generous, unique collection of white roses, lavender, and black-eyed Susans that had filled my car with a heady fragrance and now brought color to this dismal stretch of road. He collapsed beside it, head in hands. I sat down beside him. The moment I touched the earth, my breath was knocked out of me.

It was near a bend in the road, a miserable stretch of broken asphalt, close to a bunch of weeds and dying trees probably poisoned by the fumes of passing cars. Several passed us now, slowing down for an instant, but only for that. It would be easy to hit somebody if you were going fast around this bend, not stopping in time, maybe not sure what had happened. But wouldn't a person stop out of caution? Or slow down if unsure? Why had the person who hit Anna kept going?

How long had it been since she died? I closed my eyes as I'd done earlier this morning, pulling in what I could, not expecting any relief from sorrow but taking in whatever truth was there. Was there enough left of Anna's essence to sense what had happened? I called back a memory of the younger me, the one who had been present an hour after my mother's death when Aunt Phoenix and Aunt Celestine had come to say good-bye and spend time with her alone. The silence they brought with them was not just the absence of sound but deeper, darker, impenetrable; even then I knew it, as young as I was. The two breathed together, pulling in, letting go, trying to capture what was left of my mother's breath, as if they were fending off death itself. Had they done this before? I wondered. Was this a ritual that they would someday share with me? I never asked Aunt Phoenix about that evening. It still felt too personal, too private among sisters who shared only bits and pieces of themselves with me. Whatever rite they performed remained a mystery, yet something of it remained within me and I called upon it now.

I touched the ground with both hands, fingers spread wide, instinct more than anything else. This was a hallowed place that might surrender its secret. I used every sense I was given, searching, sniffing, tasting for any hint of evil. I touched one of the flowers that had been left but felt nothing. It was simply a withering bouquet left on the side of the road. I closed my eyes as tightly as I could, trying to see within the darkness of my mind any part that was left of her, anything I could touch. Then I felt something so vague, I thought it must be imagined. It grew stronger, infecting me with a sense of dread so deep and forbidding I knew what had happened to her.

"You okay?" Harley asked, alarm in his voice. Strangely enough, I'd forgotten he was there. I snatched my hands from the ground, folding them in my lap.

"Just these old bones. I'm too old to be sitting on the ground like this." I managed a smile, hoping he didn't sense what I did.

"Why don't you just go back and sit in the car. I just want to stay here a while longer, if it's okay?"

"Yeah, I think I will." I stood up slowly, weakened not by

"old bones," which I was too young to have, but something I couldn't explain.

I was certain now that evil had stalked Anna, had followed her and run her to her death. The earth where her blood had flowed told me that. That knowledge had come through the tips of my fingers, up my arms into my mind and heart. Perhaps the gift had it right. But then as usual, doubts about the reliability of my family legacy struck me again. I certainly didn't have a firm enough vision to go to the police. Maybe I should just be content with comforting Harley and keep my thoughts to myself. Maybe guilt and shame would drive the killer to come forward. Maybe the Grovesville police could actually solve the crime with leads they hadn't revealed. *Maybe.* It always came down to that. Yet there was one hard fact I knew: Somebody had taken the time to leave flowers where Anna had died. Who had that been and why had they felt the need to do it?

My aunt explained to me once that our "gift" came with a price. Because we were privileged enough to possess it, we always had to pay. The cost was to honor whatever knowledge it bestowed—no matter where it led us. When told the truth, we had to speak it, regardless of how foolish it made us sound. To keep silent was to betray not only our gift but also those who came before us—in my case Phoenix, Celestine, and my own dear mother. I considered all that while I waited for Harley to join me in the car.

He came back clutching a black-eyed Susan and pink rose close to his heart like a kid holding a toy. The black-eyed Susan brought back a surprisingly old memory that made me sigh. He sat beside me without saying anything, then turned on the radio. I always kept the dial at Darryl's favorite station, usually jazz but playing R and B standards tonight. Whoever was choosing the music must have been in the mood for love.

It wasn't something either of us needed to hear, but when I moved to turn it off Harley stopped me.

"Can we leave it on?"

"You sure?"

"Yeah. You know what, Dessa, for the first time in my life I get love songs. That probably sounds dumb, but I understand them, like everything I hear is what happened with me and Anna. Everything."

"It does take being in love to understand love's inspiration," I said, sounding foolishly philosophical.

"No, I mean, really. My mom used to play all these ole-timey singers singing old songs about love and how it changes you. I get it now. Like this one, that's playing now. Stevie Wonder talking about loving someone for always. Until the day is night and night becomes the day." Harley hummed, then sang the words in a soft, hoarse whisper.

"I wouldn't consider Stevie Wonder old-timey," I said, defensively and thinking that I shouldn't have mentioned my "old bones."

"I didn't mean it like that he's *old* old, but like he understands how love changes you forever. Nothing is the same anymore. For always."

Until you fall in love again, I thought but didn't say. I ruefully remembered my first love and how cruelly he'd left me. I thought I'd never recover and would love and miss him forever. It was the most devastating thing that had happened to me and made me believe I was doomed to unhappiness—until I fell in love again with Darryl. Harley would fall in love again, too, sooner or later, although it would take a while like it had for me and be different and deeper than he could imagine. My lost love had betrayed me in a terrible fashion, and I had found my way back to life, although the road had been bumpy with more than its share of unexpected curves.

"I'll never get over what's happened," Harley said.

"It will get easier as time passes, and when you think about Anna you'll smile, be happy, and that is no small thing." I told him what I knew for sure.

His sigh took everything out of him. "Anna left some letters and personal stuff at my place that she wanted me to go through with her, figure something out, she said. I don't think I'll be able to go through them, though, ever."

"It might make you feel closer to her. Wait a while and then go through them slowly at your own pace. They were things she must have felt were important enough to share with you. Something that was exciting or puzzling."

"Yeah, you must be right," he said, his thoughts drifting off again. "They'll never find out who killed her, will they?" he said after a while, looking straight at me for the first time since we'd been here, begging for any truth I could give.

"I don't know," I said, which was the only truth I knew.

"I feel like I owe her something, like I'm betraying her, just letting things go. Do you think I owe her something?" Again, that begging for an answer in his eyes. I told him the only thing I could.

"The two of you shared something rare; love always is. Anna knew that as much as you did. You were a gift to her as much as she was to you."

"But I owe her."

I nodded without words. I owed Anna, too, not just for Harley but for myself. The "gift" had made itself known in its own peculiar way. I knew someone had murdered Anna, and it was now my responsibility to figure out what to do about it. My gift was useful only up to a point. It could hint at things unseen, things to come, but it was up to me to make sense of what it told me. To act on it, listen to it. Beyond everything else, I owed the gift; I knew that.

I dropped Harley off at his place. He didn't say much except he needed to be alone. I knew how that felt. He hugged me before he got out as if he didn't want to let me go, which made me think again about that app he wanted to put on my phone and I decided that maybe it was a good thing after all. He walked into his apartment head hung low, as if it had become too heavy to pick up.

I went home myself and collapsed on my comforting couch with a glass of merlot, downing it quickly. When it went straight to my head, I realized I hadn't eaten much since breakfast. I went into the kitchen and made myself a tuna fish sandwich—generous with the mayonnaise, onions, celery, relish (too tired to chop cornichons), and capers—and gobbled it down, on a Bays English muffin in tribute to Julia Child. (I'd read somewhere that was what she liked.) I settled back down on the couch, mindlessly flicking through TV channels looking for something to take my mind off this day that had begun and ended so badly. I fell asleep in the middle of the local news and woke up to Juniper licking and nipping my hand, his not-so-subtle reminder that I'd forgotten his evening meal. After I'd fed him, we trudged upstairs together, him following behind me, then stretching his plump little body across the foot of my bed like the loyal pet he was.

I gave Harley a call the next morning to check on him and he told me he wasn't yet ready to come in to Risko Realty, which wasn't surprising. He asked if I could call several clients for him because he wasn't up to talking to anybody yet, and I said I would. I was dreading seeing Anna's desk and had considered working from home myself but knew I was in better shape than him.

The best way to rid yourself of dread—or anything that goes bump in the morning—is to face it down, which is what I did when I walked into Risko Realty. I assumed it would be empty, as it often was early on a Tuesday morning, but when I came through the door I stopped in my tracks. A huge blanket of roses—bright red, crimson, and burgundy—covered

Anna's desk and fell to the floor. Unlike the supermarket scentless brand Aunt Phoenix despised, these obviously cost somebody big money; the smell overwhelmed the room. Bella's cubicle was next to Anna's and she sat in the midst of the flowers, her eyes swollen from crying. Vinton sat beside her holding her hand. They looked up when I came in. Tanya, hearing the door close behind me, peeked in from her office.

"It's so sad, the saddest thing I've ever heard! I feel so sorry for Anna; she was such a special girl," Tanya said, solemnly shaking her head in what was meant to pass as an expression of grief until she added, "I just wished they hadn't mentioned Risko Realty in the newspaper. We've had enough bad stuff happen here without this adding on to it. It's like becoming the curse of Risko Realty! Anybody heard from Harley? I guess this has really flipped his world."

Stunned as usual by Tanya's lack of tact, I managed to mumble, "Doing as well as can be expected under the circumstances."

"Do you know if Louella is coming in today? We should all be together in times like this," Tanya continued.

Up until Tanya mentioned it, I hadn't realized Louella wasn't here.

"Well, the best thing we can all do is to work hard to sell houses in Anna's memory. Does anyone know if she has family nearby? If not, Risko Realty will cover her funeral and everything, like a memorial lunch or something, okay? Okay!" Tanya answered her own question. Unwilling to reveal deeper feelings, she left the room, closing the door behind her.

"Thanks, Tanya," Vinton said halfheartedly to the closed door. Understanding Tanya as we did, he knew this was the best she could manage. We had all seen more than our share of grief within these walls, and Tanya, being Tanya and as damaged as she was, was ill-equipped to handle any of it. As for the "curse of Risko Realty," besides burning more sage, and offering heartfelt greetings to the souls who lived within, I had no idea what could be done. I made a mental note to ask Aunt Phoenix again about a remedy. This latest tragedy was one too many. There had to be *something* she and Aunt Celestine could come up with.

"Where did all these roses come from?" I asked, trying to put the bad office karma out of mind.

"Too bad they just sent red; it's kind of weird if you ask me. If Tanya meant that about covering the funeral, we don't need to buy any flowers. What does red mean anyway?"

"Love," said Bella, her tone strangely subdued. "Love undying and forever."

"Tanya said they came early this morning, and that the delivery guy said they were from the Delbartons. Strange they would send something like that; maybe they didn't know what they meant," said Vinton, turning back to his laptop.

"Tanya said the Delbartons sent it? That's quite a statement," I said.

"That's what she said. Astonished me, too. I assumed Anna didn't leave there on good terms. But one never knows, do one," Vinton said, looking up with a wink.

"Do one?" I said, joking back.

"Do one. Those words are from Fats Waller, in case you didn't get it. Me and Stuart must have seen *Ain't Misbehavin'* a dozen times. Always loved that man. Both him and Fats," he said with a soft chuckle, then broke into a falsetto version of "Honeysuckle Rose" in tribute to Anna's roses that made me chuckle, too, something we all needed this morning.

"It's quite a bouquet, isn't it? But she's got the money. Nice thing to do, though. When I first saw them, I assumed it was from Harley," Vinton said.

"No, it wasn't him," I said, which brought back last night and made me wonder again about the other flowers left at the place where Anna died.

"Then I thought it might be family," he continued.

"Anna doesn't have any family," Bella said, her voice cracking. "Nobody. No family at all. She's an orphan."

Her words hung where they were, bringing us back to all that had happened.

"No, you're wrong about that, Sweetie. We're her family. She and you were family the minute you walked through that door," Vinton said gently, which started Bella crying again, and made me give her a hug, letting her know that Vinton was telling the truth. Then I went to Harley's cubicle looking for the names he'd asked me to find, and then back to my desk. Vinton pulled up a chair to join me.

"It hit me hard, when I heard about that girl dying like she did. I haven't cried that hard since I binge-watched *This Is Us* last month. How is Harley doing?"

"Not well. We probably won't see him for a while. He needs to be by himself. I'm going to make a few calls for him."

"Not a good thing, being by yourself too long. Maybe we should drop by or ask Louella to do it. They go back. I wonder where she is. I know she didn't care for the girl, so she can't be that broken up, but . . ."

"Maybe something came up at home," I said, with vague discomfort, making a second mental note to call Louella after I talked to Aunt Phoenix about the office "curse."

I turned on my computer and went through my usual midweek chores—follow-up calls, new listings, coming up with ad copy—then made myself yet another mental note to call Reset with Rosalie about a particularly hard to move property. Thanks to a market that knew no bounds, these mundane tasks were *almost* a pleasure to do. This was a sellers' market, if there ever was one. Cocky owners and eager buyers were as plentiful as grease at a Jersey diner; it was just a matter of getting the two together. Despite Aunt Phoenix's dour text about roses falling to monkeys, I was eager to do just that.

Halfway through my e-mails, I found one from Emily Delbarton asking that I call her as soon as possible. I did just that and was surprised when she answered her own phone. I considered thanking her for sending the flowers for Anna, then changed my mind. Tanya, I realized, would want to do that herself. But if I'd wanted to give thanks, Emily Delbarton didn't give me a chance. Not one to waste time or mince words, she got right to the point.

"I'm hoping that you'll be available as soon as possible to share some of your menus with me. I'm planning a . . . an event over the weekend and I need to plan quickly. Are you available today or tomorrow?"

"Yes, of course," I said.

"Do you have time later this afternoon, perhaps?"

"Yes, of course." I repeated my words without thinking twice.

"Okay, that's good. Do you mind coming to our place in Short Hills? Could we meet there, let's say around four thirty?"

"Yes, of course," I said, embarrassingly agreeable for the third time in two minutes.

"Okay, see you then." She hung up before I could say anything else.

"Well, that's interesting," I said to nobody in particular, but our cubicles being what they are, and my nosy coworker being who he is, Vinton chimed in immediately.

"Yes, of course," he said, making me wish yet again we had more privacy in these work spaces.

"That was Emily Delbarton. *The* Emily Delbarton wants to hire me to cater an event."

"Keep this up and you'll be selling food instead of houses," Vinton said.

"Please don't do it. Don't go!" Bella broke in, her voice trembling, which puzzled me until I realized that Anna's death was affecting each of us in more ways than we thought. Anna had probably told Bella something about working at Delbarton that worried her.

"It's just a job, Bella," I said, trying to reassure her. "Don't worry!"

"She got her mind on money and money on her mind. To paraphrase the great and noble Snoop Doggy Dogg. Fats Waller ain't the only one I can quote. Nothing like the promise of fast cash to take your mind off your troubles," said Vinton, ever the pragmatist. "Don't forget to thank her for the flowers."

Vinton's mention of flowers reminded me of the other bouquet placed near the spot where Anna had died. I'd read somewhere that murderers often return to the scene of a crime, and that thought came with the urgency of the promise I'd silently made to Harley—and to myself. I thought about Lennox Royal, friend, chef, former detective. It was time for some of his delicious barbecue and sharing what had happened over the last few days. I was curious to see what he'd make of it. But first there was Emily Delbarton. It was always a wise move to put business before pleasure.

Chapter 5

Emily Delbarton's house was in Short Hills, not Bernardsville, Far Hills, or some other distant Jersey place where rich folks live, love, and contentedly die. But a mansion is a mansion and Short Hills, with its 07078 zip code, was every bit as prestigious to Jersey Realtors as 90210 was to those in LA. It was also known for its celebrated Short Hills Mall, which featured everything from Neiman Marcus to Starbucks and was reasonably close to Grovesville so I could get back in time to gobble down ribs at Royal's Regal Barbecue. I'd missed lunch in my quest for suitable menus, so my mind was on ribs *and* money when I pulled up to the Delbarton mansion.

It was located in the estates area, the most impressive spot in an impressive town. Houses were few and far between and separated by enough trees to ensure a bothersome neighbor wouldn't drop by for a cup of sugar or Grey Poupon. The Delbarton house, built in the 1890s, had the charming, wasteful sprawl that marked houses constructed when lumber and labor were cheap and plentiful. It was half an acre or so from the public road and probably had at least an acre in the back, which I was sure included a three-car garage, pool, and tennis court—if Emily's tan was any hint as to how she spent her summers. I drove up the circular brick-paved driveway, pulling in front of the three-story house, which seemed to peer down on me in nineteenth-century snootiness, making me keenly aware of my Subaru's dusty appearance. The doorbell seemed to chime forever; Emily Delbarton finally answered the door.

"Thank you for coming on such short notice," she said as she beckoned me into a spacious vestibule lit by lights hanging from the domed ceiling. I followed her past several rooms, including a kitchen, filled with professional grade appliances, and a dining room fit for a banquet, into a small, sunny office off the living room.

"This place is too big for just two people," she said, as if reading my mind. "At some point when things finally calm down, I'll be putting in on the market and live full-time at my place in the city."

"It's a beautiful house," I said for lack of anything better, but wondered what things in her comfortable life could possibly need calming down.

"It's too big for two."

"Two?" She was right about that, and I didn't hide my surprise.

"Two," she curtly reiterated, discouraging any further conversation. "I told you on the phone, I'm considering giving a luncheon soon." She got straight to our business—or what I *thought* was our business.

"Thank you again, for considering me," I said, hoping I didn't sound *too* obsequious. "I've brought some menus that can work both for luncheons as well as brunches and everything in between. If you're interested in something else, I—"

"No," she said, interrupting me and grabbing my samples. "I understand a young woman who once worked for me died recently?" She asked it casually, as if it had just occurred to her. Placing the menus on the table in front of us, she glanced up, her eyes surprisingly cold and probing. I noticed again the troublesome glimmer that had caught my attention at the open house and recalled her desperate search for Anna. It struck me odd then and still did.

"Anna Lee."

"How did she die?" she asked, shuffling through the menus but seeming to barely read them. "Was it an accident?"

Sunlight drifting in through the windows suddenly heightened the impact of that glimmer. It had been bronze verging on gold that had hinted of wealth and money, but now there was the trace of another element; it had a sinister shadow that made me recall the tremor in Bella's voice.

"It was a hit-and-run. She was killed when she was jogging," I said, trying hard not to stare at her.

She went back to the menus, shuffling through them again.

"Where?"

"A road frequented by runners in Grovesville."

"That's where she lived?"

"Yes," I said, with discomfort, as if being questioned by the police.

"Do they know who hit her, any ideas about that?" She kept her voice even, as if only mildly interested, but the stiffness of her body, the way her eyes hovered around the space above my head, told me something different.

"No. But they will," I said, although I knew that wasn't the truth. It was time for me to ask some questions of my own. "So how long did Anna work for you?"

"Not long." She picked up the few menus left on the table and went through those she'd already seen.

"Can you tell me what kind of event you're planning?"

She glanced up as if she didn't understand.

"I haven't quite decided yet," she said after a long, uncomfortable minute.

I was angry and annoyed but not enough to tell her off. I recalled Vinton's crack about my mind being on my money and money being on my mind and remembered the flowers she'd sent, which softened my feelings toward her but only a bit.

"By the way, everyone at Risko wanted me to thank you for the beautiful roses you sent to the office for Anna," I said, forcing a smile. "It was very thoughtful of you."

"Flowers? I didn't send any . . . okay," she said, her gaze leaving mine as if she understood. "Okay," she repeated in the same tone as if I hadn't heard her the first time.

"Em!" someone yelled from a distant part of the house. "Emily, you down there? Emily? Emily? Emily?" he repeated in a high, singsong voice, then burst into the room like somebody making a dramatic entrance in a Broadway play.

I recognized him at once. His skin was paler even than it had been before, like a vampire, Vinton had suggested when he saw him at the open house, and that struck me now as well. He was dressed mostly in black this time, white linen exchanged for black, except for his off-white silk shirt, unbuttoned down far enough to reveal more of his bony chest than was wise. He wore what looked like a cravat around his neck, a strange addition that made him look like he'd stepped out of the same century as this house. Yet his glimmer was not as strong as it had been at the event. The color of pistachios, but paler now. The color of jealousy, envy. Ghastly green. Zombie green. He stopped short when he saw me, then came to stand in front of me, looming like a shadow.

"I know you! You were there! There that last time. At the party where I saw her. You were there!" he said, as if accusing me of a crime. Emily Delbarton must have noticed the alarm and discomfort on my face. She stood up protectively, but I wasn't sure which of us she was trying to protect.

"This is my brother, Edgar Delbarton," she said.

"This is my sister, Emily Delbarton," Edgar mimicked, in his puzzling high voice, as if I'd just walked in and he was doing the introductions. "My parents named us after poets. Me after Edgar. Emily after Emily Dickinson. Edgar Allan Poe in case you don't know who I'm talking about. My name is Edgar Allan Delbarton!"

"Oh!" I uttered the only word I could manage.

"But I'm more like Edgar than she is like Emily, right? Edgar Allan Poe," he said again as if I'd hadn't heard him. "Edgar—"

"We heard you the first time," Emily snapped.

"She's not at all like her poet, is she?" he said with a wink at his sister before turning back to me. "Why are you here?"

"What?" I was genuinely puzzled.

"Did you work with her?" he demanded.

"Who?" I said, suddenly monosyllabic.

"Annabel Lee. 'For the moon never beams, without bring-ing me dreams of the beautiful Annabel Lee; and the stars never rise—'"

Emily rose to her full height then, taller than either of us, her harsh voice coming from deep inside. "Shut up with that stupid poem. Shut up and don't say anything else. Nothing."

"She's not like Emily Dickinson at all, is she?" Edgar said teasingly. "Our parents misnamed our dear Emily. What were—"

"I told you to be quiet, please." The anger in her voice had softened and mixed with an edgy tenderness, hinting at a complex but strained relationship, but it was clear that she loved her little brother. Her eyes pleaded with me for under-standing.

"Did you work with her?" He turned toward me, his tone suddenly bullying.

"Thank you for sending the flowers. They were beautiful," I had to say something to rid the room of its tension. I knew now it was he who had sent them.

His smiled widely, bowing dramatically. "Roses. She loved roses; she told me that once. Red. Just red. That was her favorite color, did you know that? Did you find what she left for me?" He abruptly changed directions with a menacing glare that sent a nip of coldness down the back of my neck.

"That's enough," said Emily Delbarton as if she could feel it, too, speaking as much to me as to her brother. "I'm sorry to have taken up your time, Mrs. Jones. I will call you again, but I have other things to attend to now. I will send you a check for the time you've spent here." She was all business now. Her face taut, her eyes distant, and manner professional. But it slipped for a moment when she gazed at her brother. He was her tender spot, her Achilles' heel.

"That won't be necessary," I said, in *my* professional voice. "But I do look forward to working with you another time, whenever."

"Whenever," she said, her mind clearly somewhere else.

"Did you find what she left for me?" Edgar said, still standing directly in front of me, staring down waiting for an answer. I stood up, gathered my menus off the table, met his eyes.

"Anna's death was sudden. She didn't leave a message for you or anyone else." My throat was so tight it was hard to speak. The room felt as if it had shrunk, grown dark, despite the sunlight pouring in through the paned windows. Whatever was between these two sucked up all the air, leaving nothing but the cloying, frightening love between them.

"But you don't know that?" he continued, puzzled and angry, his eyes on the verge of closing, reptilian.

Saying nothing, I nodded at his sister, bidding her good-bye, leaving as fast as I could, not catching my breath until I was locked in my car. I drove fast out of that fancy driveway with its paved bumpy stones, got onto the main road, and pulled to the side unable to go farther. I had to calm myself down enough to drive.

Edgar Delbarton must have known Anna when she worked for his family. Was he the reason she quit? That greenish cast of his glimmer could signify jealousy, and what did that mean? Edgar had sent the flowers to the office. But someone else had placed some at the spot where she died. Who else was mourning Anna Lee?

Traffic was bad, and it was close to eight when I got to Lennox Royal's place. Lennox's diners were mostly working folks who tended to eat early rather than late, so I knew his kitchen was winding down. But the scent of spicy barbecue mingled with simmering greens and fried chicken, a recent addition to his menu, made me forget my worries, and I settled down at the counter. I looked around for Georgia, his young assistant cook, who usually worked the counter. She had a telling greenish glimmer whenever I came around, which bothered me the first time I saw her, but she was nowhere to be seen, and I was secretly relieved. Her feelings toward Lennox were unclear to me, and I suspected they were to him as well. I sensed she was envious of our relationship, which I found puzzling. Lennox had mentioned a while ago that he wanted to talk to me about something to do with Georgia, but he didn't bring it up again and I didn't ask.

I had no idea what was going on between them, if anything. Georgia was a pretty woman, young, with a quick impish smile, dimmed only by that glimmer, which, thankfully, nobody could see but me. I was certainly no threat to her when it came to either looks or spirit. If she was truly interested in Lennox and, more importantly, if he had feelings for her, somebody would let me know soon enough. I was in no rush to find out one way or the other.

Truth was, Lennox Royal was one of those good-looking men who had no idea how attractive they were, which made him more appealing to any woman with good eyesight and a beating heart. Yet his looks, as striking as they were, weren't what drew people to him. It was his manner and his eyes—probing, expressive, overwhelmingly kind. He listened intently to anyone who had a story to share, no matter how whimsical or unbelievable. He freely doled out advice or hot meals and occasionally money to those who needed them. He reminded me of my late husband in that way, the undying belief that everyone deserved a second and, if necessary, third chance.

Lennox never shared all that much about himself, mostly bits and pieces about his life he'd let drop over dinner (at the Chinese restaurant of a friend) or when we sat together and talked at one of the small tables in the back of his place. He was usually too busy listening to others to talk about himself. The one thing I did know was that he loved to cook, and his restaurant was more avocation than job. I also knew he was a retired police detective, divorced, and raising his daughter Lena on his own. He never shared the woes of single parenting, but I knew it was probably tough.

Lena, on the verge of becoming a teenager, was on the autism spectrum, which was how I'd met them both. Darryl worked with kids with special needs, and Lena had been in one of his classes. He'd been struck by her supportive, loving father, who never missed a meeting or chance to talk about what was best for his child. They both attended Darryl's funeral, and Lennox spoke eloquently about what a rare man Darryl was and what he had meant to him and his daughter and how much they would miss him. His words still comforted me when I recalled them. Much time had passed since that day, but they still made me smile. Lennox, coming out of the kitchen, saw my smile and grinned in response.

"Hey, that smile for me?" he said, settling down on a stool across the counter.

"You could say that."

"Thanks. Nice to see. What can I get you?" That was the first question always asked to anyone coming through his doors, and he answered it himself. "You okay with wings? Everything else is gone. How about some mac and cheese and collards, if you're up to Southern dining."

"I'm always up to Southern dining."

"Grab a table and I'll bring you a plate," he said, heading back into the kitchen.

I sat down at a table for two in the cozy dining room. Lena wasn't here today. She usually occupied a spot in the corner, close enough to the kitchen for Lennox to be there if needed yet distant enough for her to keep to herself.

Lennox returned with a plate laden with barbecued wings and the promised mac and cheese and greens, which immediately set my stomach growling.

"I barely ate breakfast, missed lunch, so clearly, audibly, I'm eager for dinner. Thanks, Lennox," I said, picking up a wing and taking a bite.

"My pleasure," he said in a way that meant it truly was.

Halfway through the greens, I looked up from my plate long enough to take a breath.

"This is good," I said, before getting back to the mac and cheese, which brought a smile from Lennox. "But I have a confession to make. I came for the food but for insight, too."

"Sure, you want some tea or coffee or something?"

"Yeah, tea would be nice," I said, which sent him back to his kitchen to come back with two mugs and a teapot, which immediately brought to mind Harley and momentarily dimmed my spirits.

"Some of these teas need to steep for a minute. Since you

got me into this herbal tea thing, I've really become a tea lover," he said, with feigned annoyance. "Something just crossed your mind; I can see it. You want to tell me what's going on?"

"Do you always read people this well?" Not for the first time, I wondered if his grandmother had passed along a "gift" along with her recipe for barbecue sauce.

"You got to read folks if you want to be a good cop. Some are easier to read than others," he said with a quick wink.

"Don't take me for granted. I'm harder to read than you think," I warned, telling the truth.

"Does this have something to do with that hit-and-run killing over on Parksmith Drive? The minute I read that the victim worked for—"

"Yeah," I said, not giving him the pleasure of saying the words. In the year that Lennox and I had become close friends, there was only one thing that we disagreed about: my continuing loyalty to Risko Realty.

"Family?" he asked, knowing the answer.

"Family."

He poured us both some tea and we sipped a while in silence. It was mint blended with chamomile. Perfect for calming the moment. I silently congratulated myself on influencing his taste in teas. He waited until our tea had cooled before speaking again, giving up on the dangers of my working at Risko Realty, but his slight hesitation told me he might be recalling something else unpleasant. "My ex-wife jogged over there. I know the spot. It's a dangerous road for a jogger or driver. There's no way to see what's coming around until it's too late. My ex-wife ran mornings, but it was dangerous then, too. I worried about her every time she put on her running shoes."

His nameless "ex-wife" was clearly a topic he was uncomfortable talking about, at least with me.

"Because of the road," I said, giving him the chance to head in another direction, which he promptly took.

"Road rage is one of the many costs of this pandemic. I see it whenever I drive down the street. People blowing their horns without reason, making illegal turns, cutting people off. They're frustrated and take it out in their cars. I've got a friend in LA says hit-and-runs are higher there than they've ever been. People there don't take buses, they drive, and driving is the problem."

"Do they ever find the killers?"

"No." Always the cop, Lennox sighed with a solemn shake of his head, what he always did when it came to unsolved crimes. "There are never any witnesses. It's done late at night or early in the morning, so there's no way to know who's done it. Always a tragedy for survivors because there's no resolution. Nobody pays the price."

I sipped my tea with a solemn sigh of my own, thinking about Harley and the loss he would always feel.

"Impossible to catch. You can't even tell if it was an accident, somebody just hit somebody and just kept going, or if it was premeditated murder," Lennox continued.

I nodded like I agreed, but I didn't. In this case I knew what it was.

"You want something else to eat?" Noticing I looked unsettled, he assumed it was hunger.

"No, I'm fine. Can I ask you something else?"

"Sure, but I'm not giving you my secret ingredient for those greens. I'll give you a hint: It's a spice you wouldn't guess."

As long as it's not nutmeg, I thought, then brought up what had been on my mind since finishing the last wing. "Just out of curiosity, how do you go about solving a crime with no witnesses?"

"Well, there are *always* witnesses. Somewhere. They just don't know what they've seen. You start talking to people who saw the victim before he was killed. If he was at a party, interview the other guests. Talk to people at work. Anyone who had contact, no matter how casual, can give you a clue. What is the unsolved case you're trying to solve?" He scrutinized me like he would a witness who didn't know what she saw. "Don't tell me; I know."

I sipped my tea, played with a bit of macaroni left on the edge of my plate. "What can you learn from the scene of the crime?"

"Sure you're not applying for a spot in the police academy?" he said with a quick grin, then turned serious. "Depends upon the crime. Where it took place, the time, when the body was discovered, there are so many variables it's impossible to say. If you're asking about that hit-and-run, there wouldn't be much left to discover. She was killed on the road, a day or more before she was discovered. It's too bad her body wasn't found earlier, maybe there would be more to learn, but it's not surprising. Like I said, I know that spot and it's hard to see from the road."

"Maybe it wasn't a hit-and-run?"

"I assume that's what the medical examiner says that it was. He could probably tell from her injuries. But they might need to get permission from the family about an autopsy. Did she have family nearby?"

"I don't know much about her, except that she was a lovely young woman. I do know when Harley and I left flowers—"

"Left flowers! You went back to the place where she was killed? Wasn't there police tape or something around the area?"

Lennox was visibly alarmed, and I felt foolish for not paying more attention to it. I hesitated before answering. "Well, we stepped over it. Harley wanted to put his flowers near where she died."

"Harley again!"

"But somebody had put flowers down before we got there, and the tape had been trampled into the ground. Do you think it could have been the driver who killed her?"

"Odessa." The use of my full name hinted I was in for some kind of scolding, but his eyes softened and his tone was one of concern rather than reproach. "Don't go back there, promise me. And be careful. Never forget that a killer is a killer no matter what he looks like or where he comes from, and he kills when cornered. If you need my help or feel threatened, promise that you will call me day or night, okay?" he quickly added.

I was touched by his words and felt a catch in my throat; I didn't trust myself to answer.

"Want some pie?" he asked, taking note of my hesitation, sensitive man that he was, and I nodded I did. Yet long after I'd left the warm comfort of Royal's Regal Barbecue and his tasty apple pie, Lennox's warning stayed with me.

Chapter 6

It was the end of a heartbreaking week I was glad to see gone. I was alone in the office. Tanya never came in on Fridays, and nobody expected her. Bella had gone to a nearby printer to pick up new business cards. Vinton had taken a leisurely lunch from which he had no intention of returning. Louella had come in earlier, said nothing to nobody, which was how it had been all week. I decided to pick up a big box of Kentucky Fried Chicken on the way home and surprise her with a take-out dinner, a sure winner with Red and Erika.

Something was bothering Louella and crispy fried chicken, with sides of fries and Sprites, was one way to pry it out of her. Louella had made no secret about her disdain for Anna, and I still wasn't sure why that was. I did know that Louella feared change; she'd had too much too quickly in her few short years. She had gotten comfortable with our office dynamics. Anna and Bella had changed the order of things. I suspected Louella felt guilty about Anna's sudden death. Ever since the tragedy of her mother, Louella wore guilt around her neck like a yoke. She blamed herself for everything—from not selling enough houses, to forgetting to buy pink ribbons for Erika's hair, to misunderstanding the depth of her mother's troubled soul. More than once, I'd pleaded for her to go easy on herself and forgive any missteps she thought she'd made. Life simply happened, I'd told her, and there was nothing you could do to change it. It was always best to look toward the future and not dwell on the past. Sometimes she listened, but often her eyes went blank as if I were talking to myself. Tonight was as good a night as any to give it another try.

I was rehearsing in my mind what I would say when the door suddenly opened, then slammed closed. I thought it was Bella coming back with her cards and didn't bother to look up. Until he spoke.

"She left me something; I know she did. She left me a message, my Annabel Lee!" It was Edgar Delbarton, his voice wheezy but threatening, more hiss than whisper. As he entered the office, he stopped to survey each cubicle. Rose petals were on the floor near where Anna once sat, and he moved toward them. Lennox's words about killers being killers, no matter what they said or looked like, came back to me, and my body went stiff. "This is where she sat, isn't it? What are all these petals? Where are the flowers I sent her? Who took away all her flowers?" he whined, glaring at me, his eyes filled with rage.

"They were dead, and we threw them away." I finally found my voice. It had been Bella who had done it two days ago, hauling them off the desk, then outside to be picked up by a garbage truck that night. She had done it angrily, stuffing the dying flowers into the black plastic bags with such a vengeance it verged on violence. Vinton and I had watched her do it in silence, then went back to work. I assumed this was simply a manifestation of her grief. I knew from experience that grieving came without rhyme or reason and you never knew how it might come. She probably couldn't take another day of being reminded of her friend and getting rid of the roses was a quick remedy. The flowers had to be thrown out sooner or later, and to everyone's relief, Bella had taken it upon herself. I wondered now if she knew more about the sender of those flowers than she'd let on and if that had been the source of her rage.

Edgar entered Anna's cubicle and collapsed into her chair, then buried his head in his hands and began to shake violently. It was an insult to have him close, so near to where Anna had once sat. I dug through my bag for my phone to call the cops. Then he began to wail with such anguish I changed my mind, touched by the depth of his pain.

"You okay?"

He shook his head like a frightened kid, his eyes big as he stared back at me as if he was afraid to speak.

"Are you okay?" I asked again, more firmly this time, demanding an answer.

"No," he said, his voice trembling. "I'm not okay."

I took note of his glimmer again; the green that I'd noticed before was now shaded with streaks of blue. Was this a sign of his sorrow or something else? Would a killer show up at his victim's workplace or send flowers? I relaxed, not as frightened of him as I'd been before.

"I just want to know if she left me a message that she'd be gone from my life. If you will just let me look around, that's all I want."

"Okay," I said, as though he were making sense. I didn't want to confront him; I still wasn't sure what he was capable of. "What are you looking for?"

He looked puzzled for a moment. "A sign."

"A sign of what?"

"Why she left me." He shrugged his shoulders and touched Anna's desk as if it were alive. Maybe it was for him. "She didn't tell me she was leaving."

"She didn't tell anyone." He'd become timid more than anything else and with each word less frightening. I was curious about what he might tell me and decided to push him some more. "Do you know how she died?" If he wasn't the one who killed her, maybe he was a witness who knew more than he thought.

He nodded his head. "She was hit by a car." He threw his head back closing his eyes as if he could feel the impact of the car, as if he were the one who had been hit. Or done the hitting. "She must have known something. She must have had a thought that would happen. She would have left me something, I know she would have, something for me, something that nobody but me would recognize."

"How well did you know her?"

He didn't answer at first, then said in a singsong, taunting voice, "'Many, many a year ago, in a kingdom by the sea, that a maiden there lived whom you may know by the name of Annabel Lee.'" He smiled mysteriously as if I should know what the heck he was talking about. I rephrased my question.

"When did you meet her?"

"We were tied together in ways you would never understand. In ways nobody could understand. Nobody."

"Like Emily?" I said, remembering his sister's reaction when he came into the room, that mixture of protectiveness and anger. How much did Emily Delbarton know about this connection he shared with Anna Lee? How far would she go to protect him?

"Yeah," he said, defiantly. "Like Emily."

He strolled around the small office, stopping occasionally to glance into the cubicles, finally stopping to gaze at the staff photo that hung on the wall. We'd taken it as part of an advertising campaign Tanya had come up with to emphasize, as she put it, our young friendly faces. It was taken a few days before Anna was killed, and she stood next to Harley, her smile beaming brightly as it always did. I gazed at her now, too, an ache piercing my heart. I thought Edgar might try to take it with him, grab it and run before I could do anything, but he touched Anna's image instead like he had the surface of the desk, as if it were flesh and blood.

"Can you tell me where she lives? Maybe she left something—"

"No. I don't know where she lived," I said, cutting him off. There was no way I was going to tell him even though I knew only too well. If I'd had my wits about me (or the gift had been working like it was supposed to), I would have warned her not to move there, but I didn't. None of us did.

Anna lived in a spacious one bedroom that came on the market a few days after she had joined Risko Realty. The market being what it was, we knew it would disappear fast. Anna had been saving money and waiting for the perfect investment; this was it. Harley handled the sale for her blithely ignoring the old adage about mixing business and pleasure. My breath caught in my throat when she told me the address. It was that gated community on the edge of Grovesville and Bren Bridge, a once upon a time sundown town. It had also been home to the lately deceased (actually murdered!) Dennis Lane, a former member of our staff who had met his bloody, inglorious end in one of the high-end apartments. None of us wanted to dim Anna's enthusiasm and we were all eager to let the past dwell where it belonged. Only Louella, for understandable reasons, had not dropped in with a housewarming gift; nobody held it against her.

"You claim to be her friend, why don't you know where she lived?" He looked puzzled, as if that had never occurred to him, then returned to his tried and true.

"She left me something; I know she did. She left me a message, my Annabel Lee."

We were both standing now, me next to my desk wondering if I could make it to the door if he made some violent move, him next to Anna's space, laying claim to it. I picked up my cell phone, finally prepared to call the police.

"You're trespassing. The office is closed. If you don't leave now I'm calling the cops," I said in the calmest voice I could manage.

Edgar cocked his head to one side as if daring me to do it, then gazed down at Anna's desk, as if still searching for something that wasn't there. Neither of us heard Bella come into the office until she began to scream.

"Get out of here! Get out!" She moved toward Anna's desk lunging toward Edgar with all her weight and knocking him off-balance. He tumbled into Anna's vacant chair, which stoked Bella's rage. She turned to me then, eyes wide and staring. "Do you know who this is? Why did you let him in? Why is he here?"

"Annabel Lee—" he said before I could answer, and she turned back to him.

"Don't you dare call her that!" she shrieked, shaking with rage.

"But that was her name," he said softly, sounding like the sane one.

"Her name was Anna. Not what you called her, that you think she was! Anna Lee, not Annabel Lee after your stupid poem!" Her voice was controlled now as she shifted forward, fearlessly confronting him. Bella was a slight, petite woman, but he cowered in fear, his head falling down to his chest.

Annabel Lee. When I'd first heard Edward call her that, I thought I'd recognized it, but now hearing Bella say the name in the context of a poem my memory was sharpened. Darryl, my English lit major of a husband, had done research on Poe for a paper. I didn't remember much about his work but did recognize the title of the famous poem. How did that poem tie Edgar to Anna?

I turned toward him with renewed interest, considering again if it was time to call the cops, then realizing in the same instant that Bella, the obvious aggressor, would be the one who would probably end up in handcuffs.

"Anna! Anna! Anna! Say her real name. Say it!" Bella loomed over him, screaming into his face, words aimed at him as if they were weapons, each assault pushing him lower into Anna's chair. It was a side of Bella I had never seen. She had always struck me as timid. Anna had the fire, unafraid to speak her mind or take on those who got on her nerves. She must have willed that spark to her friend. Cowering and bent like an old man, Edgar pulled himself out of the chair. Keeping his eyes on Bella, he backed toward the door, but she dogged his steps, daring him to say anything else.

"Now get out! You followed her here. Did you follow her to her death, too?"

"I will never give up. Never!" He left the office, too scared to look behind him.

When he was gone, Bella went to Anna's chair and collapsed. "I'm not going to cry," she said. "Anna wouldn't cry, so I won't cry either."

"I don't know about crying, but you scared the hell out of him. Just like Anna would do. You know what else she'd do?" I said, sitting down in the chair next to her.

"Laugh," Bella said.

"Yeah. She would." For a moment we both heard Anna's shimmering laugh, which always forced anyone in earshot to join.

"I really miss her. Especially at the end of the day, when we'd go out for dinner, or end up cooking at her place or mine. Fridays we'd hang out before she hooked up with Harley to spend the weekend. Friday was our girls' night, we used to joke about that. This is my first Friday without her."

"I know how that is to have a special day with somebody

who is gone and how that time will never come again," I said, my face revealing what I knew. She looked surprised when I said it, and I realized she knew as little about me and my history as I did about her. Anna and Bella had been a team from the beginning and their friendship had left little space for anyone else. Maybe that was what had hurt Louella so much, why she felt that they had cut her out. Would that change now and Bella move on?

I wondered how long they'd worked together at Delbarton and what she knew about Anna's relationship to Edgar. Had there actually been a connection or had he imagined the whole thing? What had she meant about him following Anna here and now to her death?

We sat there silent but cautiously aware of each other's presence. Bella held her face tight, still trying hard to keep from crying. I didn't know her well enough to tell her to let go and not be embarrassed to share her emotions with me. For the first time since I'd met her, I noticed a glimmer. It reminded me of the one that surrounded Anna when I first saw her. It was nearly the same lovely pink color, girlhood coming into full-blown womanhood. Something of Anna still lived within her friend, and someday I might know her well enough to tell her that. Would Anna's spirit find a way to join those of the others who dwelled within these walls? I wondered about that, too.

"Guess I better go home." Bella's tone said that home was the last place she wanted to be. "I'm still shaking from what happened with that freak. I think I'll feel better if I get out of here, pick up some dinner from somewhere, and crawl into bed."

"I know a great place to get some dinner if you're up to it," I said, thinking of Royal's, the one place in this world that always cheers me up. Lennox had a knack for making the shyest customers open up and spill out their business. He was a stranger and it was often easier to talk to someone you didn't know about what was troubling you. I'd make myself scarce and maybe he'd use his magic on Bella and she might share whatever she knew about Anna and Edgar Delbarton. "It will be my treat; come on, you'll love it. Great desserts, too," I added, discreetly tooting my own horn.

Bella thought for a moment, then finally shook her head. "No, not tonight. Thanks, Dessa, but it would just make me sad to be in a restaurant, make me miss Anna all the more."

"You don't want to be alone when you lose somebody you love. It's important to be around people with whom you can share memories, share all the things you loved about the person."

I spoke from experience. After Darryl's death, I cut myself off from friends we'd both known to the point that Aunt Phoenix and Juniper were the only sentient beings I spoke to. It was a way of shielding myself from pain, keeping anything and anyone who reminded me of the good times at bay—a form of self-destructive self-protection. "The truth is, Bella, I need some company, too," I added, telling the truth. She nodded when I said it, hinting that more than anything might help her decide.

"I don't know, Dessa," she said, suddenly having second thoughts. "I'm just not up to going to a restaurant."

"Are you allergic to cats?"

"Not as far as I know."

"Good! Then why don't you come to my house. I'm a chef, and I'll make us some dinner."

"You're a chef?"

"I cater now, but that's what I used to do."

"You sure? I don't want to be any trouble."

"Cooking is therapy," I said to reassure her.

We gathered up our things, checked the doors, and Bella followed me home. I realized with a pang of guilt as I pulled into my driveway that I'd offered the girl dinner with absolutely no idea what to cook, even though it was company more than food that she needed. Yet there were questions only Bella could answer—about Edgar Delbarton, his fascination with Anna, and how he meant to follow her to her death. And about Anna herself.

I couldn't forget Louella's crack about there being more to Anna than anybody knew. Maybe she was right. Bella had borne witness to Anna's life and, as Lennox had suggested about witnesses, probably knew more than she realized about her death. My comforting couch had a way of pulling revelations from anyone who relaxed into its cushioned folds. But it wasn't my living room that ended up pulling out confessions that evening. It was my heavenly blue kitchen—and a slapdash bowl of pasta with a spicy, notorious history.

Chapter 7

"How about some traditional comfort food?" I said to Bella, who nodded, just barely, which was good enough for me. Dried pasta keeps forever, and I went through my cabinet staples for the makings of sauce: canned plum tomatoes (good even if you don't have fresh), anchovies (first love on a Caesar salad), capers (the essential zip), oil-cured black olives (*all* olives, my fave food), garlic, and olive oil (more of both than I'll need in this life or the next).

I boiled water and sautéed crushed garlic and anchovies with a few capfuls of olive oil in my biggest skillet. After a couple of minutes, I drained the tomatoes, let them simmer, then added the olives, capers, and a toss of crushed red pepper. The spicy aroma caught the attention of Bella, who gave me a beaming smile, a hard-won sight to see.

"That's puttanesca! I love that sauce. Me and Anna had it in that new Italian restaurant that just opened up. My great-aunt says the name comes from *puta*. She would spit that word out, saying the ladies of the night, as she put it, made it to lure customers into their beds. Didn't keep her from making it, though."

I added salt and the pasta into the boiling water and sat

down across the table from Bella, waiting for it to cook. "It's quick, cheap, made in a pinch. If that's the truth, I've got to hand it to the girls; they knew what they were doing. Your great-aunt sounds like a character. I have one of my own." Aunt Phoenix would be duly insulted if I called her my "great," and she *never* judged ladies of any stripe, be they from the night or the choir in church.

"Anna cracked up when I told her that. She said she never wanted to meet my aunt because she wouldn't approve of her either."

Bella's thoughts seemed to wander, giving me time to drain the pasta, dribble some olive oil on it, and toss it with the sauce. I placed two blue-and-white pasta bowls on the table in front of us, which brought back memories. I couldn't remember the last time I used them; Darryl had been alive then. I rarely made pasta for myself and when I did I ate it off the first convenient plate.

"Why would Anna say something like that?" I said, unwilling to linger on those thoughts. "About thinking your great-aunt wouldn't approve of her?"

Bella gave a know-nothing shrug. I heaped our bowls full of sauced pasta and got out a grater for Parmesan cheese. "Hope you don't mind grating. It seems to taste better when you grate it at the table. How about a glass of wine? You can't have pasta without red wine."

"No, not me! I don't drink. Water is good. I'm a recovering alcoholic," she added quickly. "But don't tell anyone, okay, like at work! That was one of the secrets me and Anna shared."

"Okay," I said evenly but curious about the others.

We ate in silence, both of us hungrier than we realized or simply not ready to share our thoughts. Not yet anyway.

"Alcoholism was a secret that you and Anna shared?" I

asked after a while. It was awkward, but I didn't want to let it go.

Bella sank back in her chair, taking in my kitchen, pondering whether it was a safe place to talk.

"It's calm in here," she said finally, which meant that she'd decided it was. "Its being blue like this with the white cabinets, they look like they're floating clouds, like a kid's version of heaven."

"I never thought of it like that, but the color is celestial blue. My husband's choice."

"You're married? I didn't know—"

"He passed away a while ago," I said.

"I'm sorry. You are Mrs. Jones, after all."

"Don't apologize. His name was Darryl, and I like talking about him, remembering him."

"I'm dense sometimes. One of my faults. Vinton calls you Sunshine half the time or Dessa. Calls Louella Baby Doll. I don't know why he calls me Sweetie, which I certainly am not."

"Who knows where Vinton gets those names? But be flattered. Not everybody earns one. He thinks of you as family."

"Funny thing about family. Anna wasn't family, but I felt closer to her than I do to my real one."

"How long had you and Anna known each other?"

"We met at Delbarton. She was there a few weeks before I came. Anna was uncomfortable being the only Black person there and we got to be friends because I never fit in either. Same with me and Risko Realty, mostly everybody being Black, but I fit in now."

Something flickered in her eyes that she didn't want me to see.

"Want some coffee? I actually have dessert. You like cookies?" I had some chocolate chip cookies I'd made for Erika last time she was here and had the foresight to freeze for her next visit.

"Cookies?" Another hard-won smile. "Yeah, I'd like that. I stopped eating desserts because Anna was diabetic and she had a hard time resisting sweets. I didn't want to tempt her."

I added water to the kettle for coffee and turned the oven on for baking. "Was being diabetic one of Anna's secrets?" I asked it casually but was eager for her answer.

She shook it off with a half smile. "No secret there. That was the reason she was always jogging, exercising, trying to keep her weight under control. She didn't talk about it much, but Harley knew. She didn't tell him everything about herself, but she told him that."

I recalled Harley eating sweets for both of them, as he put it, at the open house and the memory brought back their happiness that day. What else had she kept from him?

When the water boiled, I added that and coffee to my French press, putting a dozen frozen cookies on the baking sheet, leaving a dozen for Erika, for whenever Louella returned. The thought of Louella brought back her distress at the distance between her and the other women. I didn't think they had been deliberately cruel, but it seemed that way to Louella. But Anna must have known Rosalie before. Her curious interest in Anna when I'd met her before the open house was unmistakable.

I chanced a glance at Bella; the little smile that appeared at the mention of cookies had dropped. I hoped some pleasant childhood memory would bring her back into the present. I let the cookies cool and put them on a plate.

"The other secrets you two had, just how serious were they?" Tension filled the space, which surprised me. I picked up a cookie and took a bite to break it.

"Just stuff we didn't want people to know, that's all," she said after a pause that seemed longer than it was.

"Like what?" I pushed to see what more she would say.

A defiantly proud smile said she was no longer ashamed of whatever it was. "I'm a drunk. Once a drunk always a drunk until you do something about it. I started drinking when I was in high school and it got bad. I got arrested for DUIs and shoplifting. I was still drinking when I got to Delbarton. Anna knew a drunk when she saw one. She made me face that about myself, helped me get sober, took me to AA meetings, basically saved my life."

"You'd mentioned before that Anna was an orphan, but was one of her parents an alcoholic?" I was trying to piece together bits of Anna's life as I got them, and seeing alcoholism firsthand was a sure way of being able to identify it.

"Not as far as she knew. She didn't really know her parents, one of the other things we had in common that made us close. We were both in foster care. My birth mother was young and dumb and, considering what happened to me, probably a drunk. I got adopted by good people when I was three. I adore my adoptive parents and they adore me. Anna got tossed around in foster care until she aged out. My natural mother was the drunk. According to Anna, hers was just nuts."

"Nuts? What made her think that?"

"Anna used to say there was something weird about her birth and how she ended up where she did but never said what it was. Her mother gave her a name, though. Annabel. Her mother's last name must have been Lee, but she didn't know for sure. Annabel Lee, which is why that freak thought she was connected to that poem. She tried to find out more about her father and did a search with DNA testing and through some site. I know it was important to her."

"Why look now?"

"She and Harley were talking about getting married and she wanted to know who her family was in case they had kids.

They were moving in together and Anna had already dropped a couple of boxes of her stuff, old letters and things, at his place. I'm pretty sure she told Harley about her search and if she had some news about her birth father, but I don't know. Harley might, though. It doesn't matter now, does it?"

"No, not anymore," I said; mentioning it to Harley now would just bring him more pain. "The obsessed freak you mentioned was Edgar Delbarton?"

She stiffened at the mention of his name and her jaws tightened. "When I saw all those damn red roses at her desk, I knew who they were from and I got sick to my stomach. I really did." Her quick glance asked if I believed her, and I nodded that I did. "I went into the restroom and threw up. You know what my first thought was? At least he can't bother her anymore. That's what it was."

Juniper, detecting as he always does a foreign presence in his space, bounced his way from upstairs on my bed to the kitchen via the living room, startling us both with a loud, intrusive meow.

"You did say you weren't allergic to cats, right?" They surveyed each other cautiously, until Bella broke the spell with a hand dangled in his direction. Juniper, sensing whatever cats do, took the hint and licked her finger.

"He's cute," she said, charmed by his antics.

"He has his days."

She patted him gently on the top of the head. Juniper turned his attention to me; staring with impatience in his round green eyes, he began mewing loudly and angrily.

"Quiet down; I'm getting your food now," I said, as he followed me to the pantry and sat patiently on his haunches as I filled his plate with food and gave him fresh water. For the next few moments, the only sound in the room was him crunching away.

"Did you know that cats never meow at each other? It's

only at their owners," I said with slight irritation as I sat back down. "That was his hungry meow. He has a whole collection of mews and cries he pulls out when he needs them."

Bella smiled, then frowned again, as if her thoughts had turned back to her friend. "Anna was getting a cat, but when she and Harley decided to move in together, she changed her mind."

"Parker?"

"Harley has a roommate?"

"No, that's his parakeet."

She laughed lightly, hinting at a good memory. "Anna used to talk about somebody named Parker who lived with Harley. I assumed it was his brother or a friend. She said this Parker person, whoever it was, took to her, too. I had no idea she was talking about a bird. But I'm not surprised. There's not a creature in this world who wouldn't love her."

"Not everybody!" I didn't realize how insensitive it sounded until it was said.

"You don't think it was an accidental hit-and-run. You think somebody deliberately killed her, don't you?" The forlorn look in her eyes made me wish I could call my words back. All I could do was tell her what was really on my mind.

"Could your secrets have had something to do with Anna's death? Maybe somebody didn't want them to get out?"

The tension that had been between us before the coffee, cookies, and Juniper's intrusion returned. It took her a while to answer. "There was big stuff like I told you before like being foster kids, and funny stuff, like having the same names."

"Same names?"

"My name is really Annabella. Hers Annabel. Bella! Anna! We both kept the parts we liked. We used to joke about it, until the freak showed up and took it to crazy land."

"How far did he take it?"

"All the roses stuff when he got her the job. Used to tick

his witch of a sister off, but she couldn't do anything about it. Anna owed him and he knew it. But so did she."

"So that's how she got the job at Delbarton. Edgar Delbarton."

"He never let her forget it either in his creepy way; that was why she had to leave. I wasn't staying there without her, so we left together. A team. Rosalie, the reset girl, was friendly with Anna, too, but we didn't even tell her. We just quit and left as quietly as we could."

Anna's relationship with Rosalie wasn't a surprise, but her tie to Edgar Delbarton was.

"Anna was scared of him, you know. I was, too," Bella added as if she could sense my next question.

"He's a scary guy."

But did he have a connection to Anna's death? Had he killed her because he was jealous?

"Do you know how they met?" I couldn't imagine where Anna could have hooked up with somebody like Edgar Delbarton. How much did she owe him? Was killing her his payback?

Bella leaned back in her chair, as if hesitating to say much more, and then her expression changed, softened as if she decided it did little good to hold in secrets that no longer mattered. "Before she came to Delbarton, Anna worked in a gentleman's club. That was her big secret."

"Gentleman's club?"

"You know, where *gentlemen* go for *entertainment*."

"You mean a strip club?"

"I didn't know the difference either until Anna told me. She'd roll her eyes and shake her head. I can still hear her voice explaining it. Cleaner tables, softer couches, better liquor, richer men. The dancers are exotic, not erotic, but it came down to the same thing. Anna would break out laughing then, you know that loud, crazy cackle of a laugh she had."

"Did she talk much about it?" A wave of sadness came over me when I thought of what she must have kept to herself.

"Not much. You know how tough Anna could be. She didn't like sympathy. The only thing she used to say was she hated their tacky name. BUNS."

"Buns?" I chuckled despite myself.

"Like maybe they served homemade buns and good coffee when they closed in the morning."

"I doubt it."

"Working at BUNS was Anna's big secret. I knew, but I don't think anybody else did. Don't tell anyone, okay?" She didn't hide her alarm at the prospect and I assured her I never would.

"I've heard worse, believe me. Everybody has secrets." Seeing glimmers, smelling nutmeg, streaks of silver running down the side of my face. Except for blood kin, I'd carry those secrets to my grave.

"Do you think Edgar tried to blackmail her about it?"

She shook her head. "In a weird way, he was protective of Anna, which was why he helped her get her Realtor's license and then got her a job at Delbarton. She was his Annabel Lee, whatever the hell that meant, and he said he needed to keep her safe."

"Safe from what?"

"Emily, I guess."

"Did she know?"

"There is nothing about Edgar that Emily doesn't know."

"But wouldn't working at Delbarton put Anna in far more danger? She'd be right under Emily's thumb."

Bella shrugged. "I don't know, but he must have thought it would be safer. That's what Anna told me anyway."

Juniper came back into the kitchen, gazed up at Bella, and began mewing loudly.

"I think he's ready for me to say good-bye," she said, and we both chuckled at that because it was getting late and probably the truth.

After Bella left, I went to our guest room, which serves as my office, Darryl's library, and Juniper's bedroom when he doesn't curl up next to me. I searched through Darryl's beloved books for his collection of poems and stories by Edgar Allan Poe. I finally found "Annabel Lee" in the poems and read it several times, once aloud, trying to figure out how it could possibly be connected to Anna's death. Darryl had scribbled some lines on the page noting that it was the last poem Poe wrote, one of adoration, loss, and memory. And that was it. There was no violence, revenge, or jealousy, simply love and grief. The only malevolent beings in the poem were "the angels, not half so happy in heaven," who sent the wind "chilling and killing" Annabel Lee. I put the book back on the shelf untroubled by the poem but disturbed by the delusions of Edgar Delbarton, who wouldn't let Anna, his Annabel Lee, rest in peace.

Chapter 8

Bella's revelations about Anna's past life at BUNS were troubling, to say the least. If Harley didn't know, it certainly wasn't my place to tell him. It was best to let Anna be remembered as the sweet, smart woman he'd known without the sordid image of her dancing on some "gentleman's" lap popping into his head. *Let Anna rest in peace,* I reminded myself, as well as in Harley's memories. Anna Lee was dead and there was nothing I could do to bring her back or change anything in her past; it no longer mattered.

Yes, there was the matter of Edgar Delbarton. Emily, a woman of considerable means and menace, would keep him in line if it came to that. His "Annabel Lee" was now out of both their lives. The wise thing to do was to help Bella and Harley cope with their grief, and go on with my life. But leave it to Aunt Phoenix to disturb my peace of mind. It was going on nine and I'd settled down to watch a Saturday night movie when she reached out with a text, reminding me of something I'd prefer to forget.

With great power comes great responsibility—Uncle Ben to Peter Parker.

"For crying out loud!" I yelled, sending Juniper scampering from his perch on the couch back to his security spot—his bowl of food in the kitchen. I immediately called my aunt.

"I see you got my text," she said.

"Yes, I did. You've gone from quoting Maya Angelou to Egyptian proverbs to Spider-Man, and frankly, I'm not sure what to make of it." I didn't hide my annoyance.

"First of all, Marvel stole those words from the Bible, Luke 12:48 to be exact, but the original was too long for me to type; my fingers get tired. I sent it because you needed reminding." I didn't bother asking how or what she knew. "By the way, Celestine's in town, and we're looking forward to seeing you. How about Monday for dinner? Celestine will cook."

"You-all are seeing a lot more of each other than in the old days," I said, pleased that they were. There had been times when they didn't see or talk to each other for years as far as I knew. On the other hand, they did have a particular way of communicating that was foreign to me.

"The older one gets, the more one treasures those who are left. Except for you and our wild cousins nobody else shares our gift. As far as we know, anyway."

"Did Aunt Celestine have anything to do with this reminder?" I didn't go into the wild distant cousins.

"See you on Monday," she said, and hung up.

"But the responsibility doesn't belong to me," I said to the empty line. It belonged to my aunts, mother, and God knew how many other poor souls who had been "gifted." How many times had my aunt reminded me that the cost of our gift was to honor the truth bestowed upon us? I had a responsibility to pay the piper, even though I didn't yet know the price. There was only one sure way to find out what that price might be, one question that had to be answered. If Anna's death was tied to BUNS, I had no choice but to go there my-self, check it out, and see what I could find.

I decided that early tomorrow morning would be the best time to visit. Weeknights were probably their busiest period so out of the question. Saturdays likely filled with night-time flyers intent upon sowing leftover wild oats. That left Sunday, the proverbial day of rest, when attendees were either lazily rolling out of bed or guiltily making their way to church. I also had to have a reason to visit. I obviously wasn't a poten-tial customer and didn't look the part of a disgruntled wife searching for her wayward spouse. Best for me to fall back on a role I knew well: baker.

Muffins are easy. They're basically cupcakes, quick to make and bake after a few well-timed turns with a spoon—too much beating ruins them. And there is an endless vari-ety—blueberry, walnut, banana, name it you can make it. I used to bake them for breakfast, always invitingly warm with fresh hot coffee. Blueberry muffins were Darryl's favorites; I liked walnuts, and I'd make a batch for each of us. Unfortu-nately, this place wasn't called MUFFINS but BUNS, and the only possible reason for me to drop by was to appear naïve enough to assume it was a bakery where I could peddle my wares.

Buns are small, sweet breads, as close to rolls as you can get. As with muffins, there are varieties—hamburger, hot dog, sesame—but I suspected they wouldn't appeal to whoever was in charge. Easter had fallen before Anna's death, and hot cross buns, traditionally baked around that sacred holiday, seemed a fitting choice. Thanks to the regular baking I do for Lennox and Erika, my cupboard had much of what I needed: flour, butter, eggs, sugar, and milk. Everything except yeast. Buns need to rise, so yeast was essential—and that was a problem. But it was going on ten, and my chances of finding yeast in

any store was next to nil. I'd need to get up at the crack of
dawn, dash out, get back home, and pray the buns rose in time
to bake. But waiting for bread to rise is like waiting for water
to boil; it's stubborn and does it on its own time.

Time to put my culinary ethics aside and remember this
wasn't a baking contest. Chances were roll, muffin, whatever,
wouldn't make a difference. Truth was, anyone who believed
a full-grown woman could mistake a strip club for a bakery
wouldn't be able to tell a muffin from a bun if it slapped him
across the face and strolled away. Bread is bread as long as it's
warm, sweet, delicious, which muffins always were.

So early the next morning I baked a dozen chocolate chip
muffins. You can never go wrong with chocolate chips, and
there were plenty left over from Erika's cookies. I pulled on a
frumpy pink suit I'd bought off a sales rack, realizing when I
got it home that I'd never wear it in the light of day; it was
perfect for this morning. When the muffins were cool, I ar-
ranged them in a straw basket lined with pink gingham napkins to match my suit and bring to mind Betty Crocker with a
seriously brown tan. Arranging my hair in a suitably conserva-
tive style (where was that damn silver streak when I needed
it?), I set out for the club.

BUNS was in a seedy section of a major city bordering
Grovesville that for better or worse was quietly and quickly
on its way to gentrification. Apparently, the owners of several
businesses hadn't gotten the word. There was a used-car dealer-
ship advertising "wrecks" for no cash on the line, and a dollar
store that was definitely good for its word. One large bill-
board advertised movies of the XXX variety, left over from
the days before cable TV, and a hotel called the Sleepaway
Inn was the kind of place you'd risk your life if you slept
away in. The club, which was located smack in the middle of
the block, was by far the most impressive building. It was a
two-story stucco structure that looked as if it had been re-

cently repainted, with an impressive circular driveway that apparently offered valet service. A red-and-white awning hung over the entrance, which led to imposing wooden doors painted to look like ebony. Two folding chairs leaned on the side of the building, meant for the valets to sit on or for customers too drunk to make it to the sidewalk. Directly above the doors hung a classy bronze plaque with the word *BUNS* in fancy script.

I pulled into the driveway, picked up my basket, pasted a toothy grin on my face, and rang the bell, an odd item for such an establishment. To my surprise, and discomfort, I recognized the man who opened the door.

"Yeah, what you want? We open at noon." He looked me up and down like I was the proverbial side of beef. Thankfully, he didn't recognize me.

He was taller and heavier than he appeared at the open house but every bit as menacing and held a plastic mug of coffee from which he occasionally sipped, swirling it around like mouthwash. There were no sunglasses today, and I was able to see his eyes, which were large and surprisingly sensitive and made me think of a sizeable but sociable animal. His long dreadlocks were twisted into a braid that fell down his back, and he was in a gray sweat suit, which fit his body loosely. I noticed his glimmer again, which had struck me the first time. It was a pale pinkish tint that lingered for a moment before disappearing and hinting that he wasn't as tough as he tried to look.

"Good morning, sir. I'm Dessa," I said cheerfully, extending a nervous hand. He scrutinized me a good minute before answering.

"Blade." He put his coffee down on a small table nearby and extended his muscular hand, completely swallowing mine, but his touch was surprisingly gentle. Just like his eyes.

"Ma'am the place is closed till noon. What you doing here this morning?"

Ma'am. Another good sign. "Well, I'm a baker and eager to find new customers. I noticed the sign on your door and thought, perhaps, this would be a great place to start!" My tone, overly enthusiastic, brought an incredulous stare.

"Huh?"

"Well, the sign does say 'buns,' right?" I thrust my basket in his direction, pulling back the napkin so he could glimpse them. "I'm looking for a new place to sell my goods and—"

He leaned back to take me in. "Ma'am. This ain't no bakery. This is a strip joint." His tone was suspicious yet sympathetic.

"Strip joint?" I said with wide eyes as if I'd never heard the words before.

"A gentleman's club to be exact."

"Oh, dear. I heard a young friend of mine used to work here. She passed away recently, and I assumed—"

"Well, you assumed wrong." He said, but then his eyes filled with concern. "Passed away recently? Only know one girl who used to work here who just died. What was your friend's name?"

"Anna Lee." I watched his reaction closely. He leaned forward as if the air had been knocked out of him.

"Did you say 'Anna Lee'?" He said her name as tenderly as I'd ever heard it, pulled out a handkerchief, and wiped his face as if he were sweating but it wasn't hot enough for that.

"You knew her then?"

"Yeah, I did. A nice kid. A real nice kid." He sat down on one of the folding chairs, pulled one out for me, and nodded toward it. Picking up his cup, he took a long sip, sighed again, then turned to me as if just remembering I was there. There was a glisten of tears in his eyes. "Hey, you want some coffee or something, ma'am? There's some inside."

"No, thank you. But would you like a . . . a . . . bun?" I stumbled over the misinformation. "Chocolate chip!"

"Chocolate chip! I love me some chocolate chips. There ain't nothing in this world, nothing I like as much as chocolate chips." He reached over, grabbed a muffin, gobbled it down, and took another.

"Help yourself," I said, unnecessarily, and he sheepishly grinned.

"Don't know when the last time was I had something with chocolate chips. Years, maybe. My auntie used to make chocolate chip cookies for us when I was a kid. Better than Famous Amos, remember him? Every time I eat a chocolate chip cookie I think about her and want to cry."

"That's nice," I said, and took a muffin for myself. He was clearly a man to whom tears came easily. We ate in silence for a while, Blade alternating sips of coffee with bites of muffin. He was on his fourth when I got around to asking the questions I'd come to ask.

"Anna told me she worked here, but she didn't say much about it."

"Nothing much to say."

"How long was she here?"

"Not long. She was a good girl, though. Only danced, none of that other stuff. Didn't do nothing special for nobody if you get what I mean." He bowed his head slightly, as if paying Anna—and me—some respect. "A dance, a big smile, that's all those losers got from Anna. But that pretty smile earned her plenty, I'll tell you that. That's one thing folks don't know about men: A pretty smile is worth a lot after a certain age. Where do you know her from?" he asked, suddenly wary.

"Real estate." I told him the truth because I couldn't come up with a lie quick enough.

"That makes sense. I heard she was going to be selling some houses. What company was that?"

"A big-time one. I sold buns and muffins during coffee breaks."

He nodded. "Delbarton. Big-time place, all right. Probably bought more than her share of buns and muffins from you, even though she didn't eat sweets. Anna was generous that way. When she worked here if she had money she tipped everyone she could—boys who parked the cars, bartenders, even me, but I never took it."

"Do you know why she left?" I was eager to get Blade's take on it.

"Edgar Delbarton. Him and his sister."

"Emily Delbarton?"

"That woman has the last say about folks who works here and folks who don't, and she had it in for Anna because her nutcase of a brother had the hots for her. She made it uncomfortable around here for Anna. That's what boss ladies do, right?"

"Boss lady?"

"That's what I said."

"How did she make it uncomfortable?"

He took a quick sip of coffee. "I ain't saying no more."

"You don't mean to say that Emily Delbarton, who owns the real estate company, also runs this club?"

He studied me hard, as if trying to figure out what I knew, then shrugged his shoulders as if deciding that anyone showing up at a strip club selling buns probably didn't know much of anything.

"She doesn't run it; she owns it. With some unmentionables who I won't mention. You know who I'm talking about. We all knew it, even Anna. But I heard that despite what his sister wanted, the nutcase got Anna a respectable job at his family's firm. I don't know how that sat with big sis.

Maybe he got it to keep her quiet. Keep an eye on her. For all I know, maybe he was trying to keep her safe. Bad things can happen at a place like this. A fancy real estate business, Anna would be safer there."

"From what?"

"If you don't know what I'm talking about I'm not going to tell you," he said, his eyes shifting away from mine.

I was the one who paused now, unsure if I really wanted to know and deciding that maybe I didn't. He continued anyway.

"I went over to some big party the Delbartons were at to make sure Anna was okay, but she ran out before we could talk. Then she was dead."

Anna had been running from somebody that afternoon. I assumed it was Edgar, but could it have been Blade? Or Emily Delbarton, who had been looking for her, too? Blade turned away from me and slipped on his sunglasses, the dark ones, and I couldn't see his eyes. "Some woman came around here looking for Anna a while ago. That's what I heard anyway. Emily Delbarton never set foot in this place in person, but she knew people who would."

"You never saw the woman?"

"I wasn't here, so I didn't see her. Just something I heard. Don't know how she looked, so don't ask me. They don't know yet how Anna was killed, do they? Who ran her over," he said, an abrupt change of direction. "Delbartons had something to do with it. I'd bet my life on it. Anna was smart and that fool of a brother told her more than he should have about the family business."

Blade pulled a handkerchief from his pocket, cleaned smudges off his sunglasses, quickly slipped them back on. It wasn't a secret how Anna had died, but nobody had been arrested, and I doubted if anyone ever would. I wondered if he could be right. He finished his coffee and eyed the few muffins that were left.

"Do you want to take some for later?"

"Don't you need some as samples?"

"Take as many as you want. I need to bake some more anyway." It took him less than a minute to grab what was left and go inside. I assumed our talk was over, but he returned a few minutes later to fold up the chairs—a not-so-subtle hint that it was time for me to be on my way as well. "Thanks for the buns. They really hit the spot."

"I think you should tell the cops your suspicions about the Delbartons."

"I ain't no fool. I value my life."

"It might help them figure out who killed her."

He shook his head. "Nah, me and cops don't get along too tough, and if the Delbartons were involved they already know it. I feel bad for Anna, though. I made her a promise I can't keep and I don't like breaking promises."

"What did you promise?"

"I'd get even with whoever did her like this. I told her that when I laid flowers at where she died. She was dead, though, guess she couldn't hear me."

"She heard you." Surprised I spoke with such certainty, Blade took off his sunglasses to stare at me for a second look.

"You sound pretty sure about that."

"I'm sure because I know," I said, not about to tell him how.

He smiled then, the first time he'd done that since I'd been there, his grin wide and friendly. "Okay, Miss psychic, no-nothing, bun-making lady. I'll take your word for it." He slipped on his sunglasses and went back inside, closing the door behind him.

When I left I noticed that a black pickup truck the same color and model as the one I'd seen at Anna's death site was parked a few blocks from the club. I figured it was Blade's and that he was the one who had left those flowers. I only had his word on what their relationship had been, and that it hadn't been him that Anna was running from when she left that room in such a hurry. Yet I trusted this "gangster" of a man who hid tears behind a handkerchief and wept when he remembered his aunt's chocolate chip cookies.

Chapter 9

I called Harley and Louella before I left for work the next morning. Anna had been dead less than two weeks, and I hadn't had a decent talk with either of them. Louella had dropped into the office for short bursts of time, but our conversations were brief and distant. Something continued to trouble her that she wasn't ready to share. I was sure it was connected to Anna.

Harley called to tell me that he'd begun going through the things Anna left in his apartment. There were some unopened letters marked "Return to Sender" dated close to the time she died, but he couldn't bring himself to open them. It seemed an invasion of her privacy even though she was no longer there. He was packing up her clothes and sorting items slowly, piece by piece, and I knew that I was right; it made him feel closer to her. He had once told me that shaking off pain, as he put it, was harder since his tours in Afghanistan. Anna's death was a wound that wouldn't easily heal, and his understanding of why she died was crucial to his healing. Thanks to my aunt's Peter Parker moment, my responsibility in finding that answer loomed large in my mind.

Bella had texted me late Sunday to ask if I would drop by

the Reset by Rosalie office and pick up some brochures on the way to work. She and Vinton had houses desperately in need of "resetting," and there was nothing like a black-and-white "Before" and colorful "After" photo to convince a penny-pinching seller that a staged house would double the profit. I'd pick up some for Louella as well; it would be a good excuse to see her. While I was there, I'd find a way to "politely" question Rosalie about Anna and about Emily Delbarton's real estate holdings. If Blade was telling the truth about BUNS, it was probably common knowledge. I wanted Rosalie's take on Edgar Delbarton, too; his unforgettable presence would have definitely left an impression.

Rosalie's office was located on an upscale street in Bren Bridge known for its affluence and history, which I could never forget. When I was a kid, my father was stopped more than once for "speeding" (which he never did) or "burned-out taillights" (which they never were). But he knew that it was really for that old dependable DWB (Driving While Black) and there wasn't much he could do about it but come home and have a cold beer. Times had changed, according to the town leaders. Everyone was welcome despite the dubious past, and there was a good mix of people of all kinds and hues. Yet my hackles went up whenever I crossed the city line, and I wondered why Rosalie would choose to do business in a place with such a sordid history, at least as far as Black folks were concerned. I suspected her choice hinted at the kind of clients she hoped to attract and, despite her invitation, Risko Realty was not among the chosen. I tried to put my doubts out of my mind as I parked my car and headed, self-consciously, down the street.

Her office was in a beauty of a Victorian, pale yellow with ornate white gable trim, bay windows, and an elaborate tower. A small tastefully lettered sign hanging in the foyer indicated that Reset by Rosalie was on the main floor. A narrow stairway going upstairs probably led to a pricey floor-through apartment. Despite my misgivings about Rosalie's choice, I was struck by what must be her considerable business acumen. Building a small business is tough, and to make enough money to pay the lease on this property took talent, discipline, and luck.

Darryl and I had dreamed about owning our own restaurant someday. We planned to start with a food truck expanding D&D Delights and go on from there. It was one of our favorite dreams, like our fantasy garden of flowers and vegetables, that never came to fruition but were fun to imagine, and we did that in abundance—and that was the memory popping in my mind that made me smile as I walked down the street. My first impression of Rosalie had been unfavorable. She had struck me as snobby, pretentious, and a bit mean. Yet success comes with personal sacrifice, and I had no idea what she had given up to achieve hers. She was the same age as Bella and Anna yet was clearly thriving in her self-made business. Slightly ashamed of judging her so harshly, I decided to sing her praises extravagantly when she opened the door. I stopped short just before ringing the bell.

The voice that came from inside was not that of the refined woman I'd met nearly a month ago. It was filled with quiet rage and such loathing it sounded like a growl.

"You're a selfish fool, if you make that donation. It belongs to me, not just to you. If you give away what is rightfully mine, I will never forgive you! Your grandmother is dead. You owe her nothing."

Who was she arguing with? I leaned closer and was able to make out a murmur of a voice, which belonged to an older man overpowered by her youth and strength. She waited for a moment, taking in whatever he had to say, then started up again in a nasty, wheedling voice.

"How could you do this to me? I'm all that's left of you. Give it all away. Your life is ending. Mine is just beginning! You know that as well as I do!"

Her cruel words stunned me. Something hit the floor and shattered, a glass or plate, easily picked up and hurled for effect. It was the ugly response of a spoiled child not getting her way, not that of a supposedly educated, sophisticated woman. The sound of that breaking glass and the spite behind it was chilling. Who was in that room with her? Was he in danger? Should I ring the bell, forcing them to stop this argument, or simply leave?

There was silence before either spoke, and when he did it was in a soft, gentle voice, one that sounded as if he was used to calming her down. I knew then that whatever this was, it was not new to either of them; they had played this out before. The room turned uneasily quiet.

"I'm leaving." Her voice became that of the cultured young woman she'd been when I met her. "But know this, Daddy: I will not let you ruin my life again," she added, ruining that impression.

Daddy! He was her father. I heard her coming toward the door, and quickly turned to make my way back outside. Whatever this family business was, it was personal and humiliating for all of us, especially me, the invisible listener. When she finally opened the door, her face was so changed I barely recognized her. Her expressionless eyes told me she didn't recognize me either.

"Excuse me," I stammered out. "I'm Dessa Jones from Risko Realty, stopping by to pick up some brochures. I'm so sorry; I can come back."

Her glimmer was burning red, an angry color I hadn't been able to distinguish before, her fury and disappointment so thick I could feel it in my throat. We stood there caught between the doorway and stairs until she edged me out of the way running upstairs so fast she risked tripping. I stood slack-jawed at the still-opened door too stunned to move.

"I'm sorry you had to hear all that," said the man from inside. "My daughter has a temper she can't control. Been like that ever since she was a baby. Blame me, not her, the overly indulgent father who loves to spoil his only child." He sounded familiar, but I couldn't place him and felt a sense of dread I didn't understand. "We're partners, me and my Rosa. I own this place, business, and a lot of other stuff that I don't like to mention, which may be part of the problem. Overprotective father, overprotected daughter, forgive us both," he added with a chuckle that sounded forced. "Come in. It's nice to meet one of our customers. Rosalie keeps me hidden from the general public."

"Thank you. I'm not a customer yet," I said, then stopped short. I didn't recognize him at first. His skin was sallow, sagging, and his hair too sparse and gray for a man his age. He was thin, wasting-away, dying thin, which made his daughter's words about his life being over and hers beginning particularly cruel. I felt a tug in my heart at the harshness of them, though God knows why I did.

"Terrence?" It came as a question because I wondered how it could be him after all these years. "Terrence Davis!" I managed to say his full name despite the feelings that churned inside.

"Odessa." He called me by the name I rarely hear. "Odessa . . . Jones? You're married now?"

"Yes."

"This is fate, answering a prayer I didn't know I'd prayed. It's been a long time, hasn't it." He headed for a couch in the far corner of the room and collapsed. He was tired; I could easily see that. His argument with his daughter had taken its toll. "Will you sit down with me for a while? I'll get the things you need before you go. It's just so good, a miracle, to see you!"

I sat down, nearly collapsing myself from surprise; there was no polite way to refuse.

"You're, wow, you're as beautiful as you've always been, as I remember you being."

"That was a very long time ago."

"Odessa—"

"Please call me Dessa," I interrupted him.

"But I always loved *Odessa*. Such a beautiful, lyrical, old-fashioned name. One you don't hear much." He called up a history I wasn't eager to remember.

"I go by *Dessa* now," I said more sharply than I intended. "Only my aunt and close friends call me Odessa."

I wouldn't have recognized him if he'd knocked me over on the street. We'd been in our twenties when we met, me just twenty, he two years older. It was the first time either of us had really fallen in love and we were overwhelmed with craziness and passion and young enough to believe our lives would turn out the way they did in movies. We'd fall madly in love. Get happily married. Have babies. Grow old together. Die in each other's arms. And then he disappeared from my life and our future, suddenly and with no explanation. Terrence Davis was my first lesson in abject sorrow and humiliation. As I sat across from him, I wondered what ironic twist of fate had brought us together again. I've never been good with painful confrontations. Given a choice between fight and flee, I'm gone in a heartbeat. I sat there, mute, unable to find the words I wanted to say.

Terrence, on the other hand, had always been good at filling uncomfortable silences and quickly filled this one. "This is some kind of serendipity, I think that's what they call it, you showing up here like this, when I most needed to see you, to make amends, to ask for your forgiveness. It must be fate."

"So Rosalie is your daughter?" An obvious, unnecessary question.

"Yes." His eyes left mine, making me wonder what they were hiding. "I know she's possessive, spoiled. Especially since— Well, that's a discussion for another day." His eyes shifted, again settling back on me. "I didn't think I'd ever see you again; I've always wanted to tell you what happened. Needed to tell you. Before I leave this earth."

"There's no need for that; the past is the past," I said, standing and ready to leave.

"But the past is never the past; you know that as well as I do." He was right; I knew that only too well. "Can you stay here a bit longer? Please."

It was his eyes more than anything else that held me, begging me to stay and listen. Maybe I still needed an answer about that time, which had thrust my innocence and young life into turmoil. I sat back down on the couch, wary of trusting him but noticing again how fragile and weak he had become. He'd been robust and muscular then, and unbelievably handsome, at least in the eyes of a twenty-year-old still foolish enough to judge men by their looks. He was also smart, determined to make money so we would be rich, he used to say. If this space was any indication, he'd achieved his goal.

The three rooms featured high, stylish ceilings, flawless wood paneling, and elaborate chandeliers spreading diffused flattering light. But as with the Delbarton property, it was the artwork displayed on the walls that captured me. There were drawings and prints by artists I recognized; I moved closer to view and admire them.

"I saw this work in a home your daughter was staging," I said, remembering the abstract by Romare Bearden that had caught my attention.

He chuckled. "It was actually a copy of that piece, a good copy but a copy nevertheless. The original is on loan to a small museum. I'm collecting work by extraordinary Jersey artists now, Ben Jones, Janet Taylor Pickett, Bisa Butler. Over the years, I've managed to get more work on paper, Bearden, Lawrence, an abstract by Norman Lewis, and Cortor, and added them to my collection. My daughter would love to get her eager little hands on all of it."

I was surprised by his words. "Eager little hands?"

"Artwork by Black artists is now considered one of the best investments you can make. I collect everything I can these days, pearl-handled antique guns, vintage cars, first editions; I've got the collecting bug, but art will always be my first love. I get calls every day from dealers representing clients who want to buy work they know I own. I'm getting a minor reputation as a collector. But most of the work I own, work on paper, oils, collages, is loaned to museums, where people can see it; I keep work that has become extremely valuable in art storage facilities in New York and Newark, which is close, so I can visit when I want to. Like family. The artists and their work are my family.

"Rosalie violently disagrees with me; you heard that earlier. She wants to put it all up for auction while the market is hot, and she's gotten major interest from greedy dealers and auction houses. But art should be seen and loved by as many folks as possible. Not kept on some rich person's wall. It's for kids who have never seen a painting before and never would. Remember when I started collecting," he said, standing to join me. "I've always had what they call a good eye, and much of what I've collected has quadrupled in value. But it's never about the money."

I nodded, remembering that he was an accountant by trade and worked for a while at an investment firm as a financial analyst. "A good catch; you'll never be broke," Aunt Phoenix, always practical, observed more than once. He was good with money, but his true love was art, and he spent days visiting emerging artists in their studios, buying what he could and paying for months for work he fell in love with. Artists appreciated his generous support and undying belief in them. They also knew they could count on him for money if they needed help. His love was as much for the creator as the work itself. Family, as he put it. I knew from my own experience that family came however you could claim it.

"I'm honoring my grandmother. Each piece I buy reminds me of how much she loved and collected art. I fell in love with it through her. She took me to lots of museums, but the one I remember most was the Hampton University Museum when I was eight. That was when I saw Tanner's *The Banjo Lesson* and didn't want to leave. Stood there for half an hour just staring at it. Maybe it was the devotion that old man showed to the kid and the fact I never knew my father, but I fell in love with that painting and all art after that. My grandmother fed that interest in every way that she could."

"Yeah, I remember you used to talk about that," I said, recalling when we'd met at an exhibition at the Studio Museum and found we lived in the same apartment building in East Orange. He'd moved up from Philadelphia and my father had just moved me into my first apartment.

"I'm glad you've found a way to live your dream." I hadn't meant it to sound as snarky as it did.

"Thank you," he said, ignoring the snark. His wistful smile brought back for an instant the young man I'd loved, that memory softening my feelings. "But it's really my grandmother's dream. She was inspired by the educator and collector Constance Clayton, who she greatly admired. They were both graduates of the Philadelphia High School for Girls, although my grandmother was years behind her, and she was immensely proud of that school. Dr. Clayton and her mother, Willabell, collected the work of Black artists, then donated their collection to a museum for everyone to enjoy; that's exactly what I want to do. I'll call it the Evelyn Davis Collection to honor my grandmother. Nothing will be sold to private collectors or dealers."

I remembered Evelyn Davis as a robust, serious-minded woman, the hardworking principal of a tough city school who smiled at the mere mention of her beloved grandson, raising him single-handedly and pouring her life into him. She was as happy as we were when we told her of our plans and determined to play a welcomed role in our lives. He'd betrayed her too. Terrence had a lot to atone for; I was the least of it.

"How is your family?" he asked, changing the subject. Perhaps talk of his grandmother made him uncomfortable.

"Aunt Phoenix is fine; you remember her, right?"

"My grandmother died a while ago." His voice was suddenly that of a boy who had lost the center of his life. "But we were able to have some good times together, and I was able to ask for forgiveness for everything that happened, for disappointing her like I did."

"And she forgave you?"

"Yes."

"Well, I guess I better get those cards and brochures and be on my way," I said, the space between us uneasy again. He gently but firmly grabbed my hand before I could go.

"I need you to forgive me, too," he said, his gaze holding mine. "I need to explain to you what happened, Odessa, because I'm dying, but you know that, don't you?"

It was clear to anyone who saw him. The sound of Rosalie's footsteps stopped whatever he was going to say. The sigh that left him seemed to take what little life he had left with it, but then he took in a breath, perked up. "Will you come to dinner at my house? We can talk then."

"That's not necessary. I—"

"Please, Odessa. I need for you to understand, to come clear about things that I should have told you years ago. I know how much I hurt you and everybody. This Friday? Please come so we can spend time together. Kind of for . . . well, for old times' sake?"

"Those old times are gone forever, but I'll get back to you about dinner. Fridays are always busy, and I may have a commitment." That was an absolute lie. Fridays were always free, but I needed time to think this thing through.

Rosalie opened the door and came back into the room, her face puzzled when she saw me. Terrence stiffened, apparently well acquainted with his daughter's moods.

"I'm so sorry, Daddy," she said, her voice cracking, her face crumbling as she buried it into his thin chest. "I didn't mean what I said earlier. None of it. You know that, right? Please tell me you forgive me, okay?"

Terrence kissed her forehead, the understanding, forgiving father. "This is a terrible time for both of us, darling. You are my daughter, and there's nothing you could say or do that I won't or can't forgive. Ever."

She hugged him again, then pulled back, noticing me as if for the first time. "Please forgive my bad manners. But we've met before, haven't we? You catered the Delbarton open house."

"I knew Odessa Jones before you were born, when her last name wasn't Jones," Terrence said before I could answer. "We are old friends. She was the love of my life." His words startled and surprised both of us. My first thought? *What about her mother?* That may have been her first thought as well. Yet I simply let those words float, not reacting to them as I studied my old love and his volatile daughter. Terrence Davis remained an unturned stone in my life. Maybe it was time for me to look underneath it.

Chapter 10

That unturned stone felt like a rock by the time I got to Aunt Phoenix's house for dinner. The sight and sound of Terrence Davis had brought back insecurities and uncertainties I thought I'd buried long ago. I wondered if my aunts might have some extrasensory solution—balm, incense, herb—that could be rubbed, burned, swallowed, anything to erase that painful time and get this uninvited man out of my life. That was my first thought when I walked into my aunt's unlocked house. The second was why the heck she hadn't locked her front door.

My aunt lived in a neighborhood once considered questionable, but now, thanks to the booming housing market, it had become highly desirable. Fixer-uppers, in dire need of a slap of paint or new gutters, were selling in the mid–six hundreds. Even my aunt had been offered a ridiculous sum for her neat, well-maintained Cape, which she quickly, rudely refused. "At these prices, where else can I afford to live? I'll stay where I am, thank you," she wisely observed. Yet still I worried about this forgetful senior woman as stubborn as she was self-reliant.

"Aunt Phoenix, someday soon an undesirable, uninvited

person is going to walk through that unlocked door, and it will be the end of you!" I called out as I entered the living room even though I couldn't be sure she heard me. My two aunts sat next to each other like reigning queens on the paisley-covered couch, the only burst of color in an otherwise spotlessly white living room. They were sipping gin and tonics and communicating silently as they were occasionally known to do.

Celestine, finally noticing I'd entered the room, looked up and grinned. Aunt Phoenix, not one to waste a precious smile, bowed her head in silent greeting. I sat down across from them on the uncomfortable ancient bentwood rocker and began to noisily rock, my childish way of entering their voiceless conversation. Studying them intently but lovingly, I contemplated what was left of my precious, dwindling family.

Except for distant cousins, unknown yet often mentioned for their heralded gifts far greater than my own, Celestine and Phoenix were the only blood relatives I knew and a striking study in contrasts. Phoenix was wearing one of her blossomy, oversized kaftans that made her look twenty pounds heavier than the lightweight she was. It was a dark green number generously dotted in white roses with magenta stems. She had slipped on her favorite house slippers, the ones made from alligator skins, which I suspected were chosen to irritate Celestine, a self-proclaimed animal rights activist. Phoenix's fingernails were painted a startling hot pink, and one of her many wigs had been abandoned. She was hatless, soft white hair encircling her walnut-brown face in a glorious halo, though angel she was not.

Celestine was camera ready as usual—rouge, lipstick, perfectly shaped black eyebrows (a la Joan Crawford in *Mommie Dearest*). She was decked out in a classic green shirtwaist dress, the identical color of her sister's, topped off with pearl stud earrings. She'd dyed her meticulously pressed bone-straight hair a flattering shade of light brown successfully camouflaging any stray, unruly white hairs, the kind in which Phoenix reveled.

After a lengthy silence, I risked starting a conversation. "So what's for dinner?" In response, the two glared at me—the rude teenager best seen rather than heard (and in this case I wasn't sure about best seen). "I was invited to dinner, right?" I continued, *not* to be cowed.

"We were waiting for you to get here so we could order," Aunt Celestine said sweetly.

"Order? I was told you were going to cook!" I didn't hide my surprise. "If I'd known I would have picked up something rather than have you spend the money."

"By the way, in response to your earlier comment, you know as well as I do that only the invited get *through* my front door," said Phoenix, pointedly ignoring my question about who was doing the cooking. "And money is no object. I just won something from the lottery. What do you want, Thai or Mexican?"

"Mexican sounds good!" I could almost taste the guacamole and chips.

"Mexican gives me gas," said Phoenix.

"Then why the heck did you ask me?" I said, almost a snap.

"Somebody is in a testy mood this evening," said Celestine.

"Somebody who has been patiently sitting in a room full of elderly women talking to each other through their minds!"

My aunts glanced at each other and then at me. "And who are you calling elderly?" said Phoenix with a raised eyebrow, daring me to tell her. In response, I simply rolled my eyes.

"Sorry, darling," cooed Celestine, the only person with the exception of Vinton to call me that endearment. "We didn't mean any harm; you know how much we love you!"

"You have a strange way of showing it. I'm sorry I was rude. I've had a hard day. And I'll have whatever the two of you are drinking. By the way, Aunt Phoenix, when did you trade your cherry brandy in for gin?"

They chuckled as if sharing a secret joke, then turned serious. "We always have a gin and tonic when we haven't seen each other for a while. Rosemary loved a cold gin and tonic in the heat of spring and summer, and we drink it in memory of her," said Celestine.

"Except winter. She drank red wine then to warm her up," Phoenix added, clarifying for the first time my undying love of red wine no matter what the season. This was one of the little things I'd just found out about my mother, and there were many bits and pieces I desperately wanted to know. My aunts took knowledge of her life for granted—but because she was gone before I was full-grown I knew her only from childhood memories. I desperately held on to everything now, no matter how trivial. Her death coming as early as it had was one of the things that may have contributed to my falling in love with Terrence Davis so quickly and completely. He'd filled a gap I now understood had been impossible to fill.

"Thai it is; tell me what you want, then I'll make you a gin and tonic, so we can toast dear Rosemary and wait for our food," said Celestine, handing me a menu, taking charge before heading into the kitchen to order. "I brought my own gin this time," she added with a critical glance at Phoenix, who pursed her lips. "And after dinner, you will tell us about your day."

"What we don't already know," muttered Phoenix. I knew she was right.

We ordered stir-fried eggplant with basil along with chicken curry and Thai salads with tofu. Despite the chili peppers in the curry, nobody complained about the spiciness. Celestine made a pot of green tea that she said was good for digestion as well as focusing your mind to think clearly, to which Phoenix added a splash of cherry brandy to "hasten" the effect, and we settled down on the couch and in the rocking chair to enjoy it. Suddenly Celestine slammed her cup down on the coffee table and glared at me.

"Where is it? You wouldn't need our help if you wore it like you're supposed to. That is your mother's protection against harm. That's why I gave it to you," she said, not concealing her irritation.

It took me a moment to realize she was talking about the amulet. "Oh Lord, I must have forgotten it," I said, unconvincingly.

"She doesn't wear it like she should," scolded Aunt Phoenix as if I weren't sitting across from them.

"I'm sorry. It's heavy; it pulls on my neck. I just never remember!" There was no sense in lying to women who would immediately know the truth. I felt a flash of guilt because the blue lace agate was one of the few things I'd inherited from my mother. I'd worn it faithfully for a while, even though it grew heavier by the day. Life seemed to be going so well it seemed the only protection I needed was from myself—too much pride, too much spending, too many blueberry scones. I certainly should have slipped it on before dropping into BUNS, but as it turned out, I didn't need it. Yet my aunts missed its presence. I needed to wear it when they were around.

"I will remember from now on," I solemnly said, all but crossing my heart.

"Please do," said Celestine.

"Because you're going to need it," added Phoenix.

There was a strained lapse in conversation; Phoenix broke it. "Never trust a man with a weak chin. A weak chin indicates a weak, cowardly man," she said with absolute certainty, one of the many criticisms she'd hurled at Terrence after

things went south. Funny thing was, I'd never noticed his lack
of a chin before she mentioned it. His roundish baby face had
been one of the things I found charming and loved about him.
Chin or no chin.

"Are you talking about who I think you are, after all these
years?" said Celestine, narrowing her eyes. Phoenix scrunched
her lips into a grim, angry line.

Celestine turned to me. "I take it that he is part of the terrible day that called for that gin and tonic. Tell us how and
why that man has shown up again in your life after leaving like
he did at the altar twenty years ago."

"Well, it wasn't exactly at the altar. It was a week before."
I said like it actually made a difference. To my surprise, I realized it was still embarrassing, even after all this time.

"I know good men who would have shot him for less.
They'd call it protecting a woman's honor. But only for those
women among us who have honor to protect," said Celestine,
unable to resist a swipe at her sister.

"The problem with the men you know who would defend a woman's honor is you allow them to define the meaning of honor. And we both know where *that* can lead," said
Phoenix with a cutting glance.

"Let's not go there in front of the child," said Celestine,
sounding weary.

"Damn it! I'm not a child! I haven't been a child for
decades!" I said, disgusted with both of them and realizing that
this was not the first time these two had had a painful conversation about past lovers come and gone and the meaning of
honor.

"But you were a child then," said Celestine, allowing
Phoenix the last word and bringing things back to me. "The
nerve of him disappearing like a phantom the week before
your nuptials after your poor father had sent out all those invi-

tations, rented that hall, hired the caterer. To say nothing of me and Phoenix doing all the stuff we had to do."

"What kind of stuff did the two of you have to do?" I asked uncomfortably.

"The usual stuff." Celestine gave Phoenix a furtive glance.

"Just what kinds of spells, herbs, and stuff were the two of you planning?" I wasn't about to let it go.

They glanced at each other, then back at me, and shrugged. "Never you mind," said Celestine.

"Rosemary was dead only a couple of years. You'd just turned twenty-one," said Phoenix, changing the subject altogether. "And then for you not to hear from him again. There's no forgiving that!"

"The point is I don't know what happened. Besides that, he was only a few years older than me. We were both kids!" I said, wondering as I spoke why I felt the need to defend him.

Phoenix loudly, rudely sucked her teeth. "But you were the vulnerable one, the one who was healing from her mama's death!"

"Maybe he was healing from something, too. I don't know!"

"But he hadn't just lost his mother, and you never fully recover from that!"

Aunt Phoenix's words rang true. Had they lost their mother, too? I wondered, not for the first time, about my grandmother, their mother, the one they never talked about, grandmother as well to the mysterious wild distant cousins. She was a presence in all of our lives. Why did they never mention her? That was a subject I'd need to explore with the two of them in another time and space. But Phoenix was speaking the truth tonight. I would always be healing from my mother's early death. The gift may have told Celestine and Phoenix that their beloved sister was going to die, but it left me out of the mix. For the second time in as many weeks, I considered the ceremony the two had performed when she died, and how it had come back to me, as instinct, when I'd visited the place where Anna died. It was yet another un-turned stone in my life I'd need to attend to.

"Just how and when did this chinless wonder come back into your life?" said Celestine, pulling me back into the present.

"Happenstance," I said, unwilling to go through the de-tails.

"There is no such thing as happenstance!" said Phoenix. "Things happen for a reason. What excuse did he have for showing up after all these years?"

"I think he may be dying and wants to come to terms with things he's done. He may just need somebody to listen to him."

"Ah! The old time-to-make-amends card! That always turns up at the end of the game. Shame on him if he hasn't found somebody to listen to him after all these years. Why should you believe anything he has to say?" said Celestine.

I paused before answering because up until that moment I wasn't sure myself.

"I need to know why he did what he did. It's not for him but for me. I loved him and I know he loved me. It was the first time either of us had fallen in love and there has to have been an explanation."

"Love, whatever you want to call it, changes depending on your age. What passes for love at twenty won't make the grade a decade later. You found love again with a man who was a gift to us all. Consider yourself lucky, count your bless-ings, forget about the past, and celebrate the present you had with a good man," said Phoenix, her wistful expression re-minding me how much she'd loved Darryl.

"But like you said before, Aunt Phoenix, there is no happenstance. What happened with Terrence is a stone I need to turn over."

"Most likely, you'll find worms," said Phoenix.

"Or rotting weeds," added Celestine.

"But remember this, Odessa. Once you turn it, you're stuck with it. You can't pretend you didn't see it, can't forget what was there. It's best to let sleeping dogs and unturned stones lie where they are," Phoenix warned.

"I need to turn this one over. Worms, weeds, whatever, I need to know."

Nothing more was said about stones, worms, or weeds as we quietly sipped our tea. Celestine awkwardly broke the silence. "So how is Parker these days?"

"Parker?" I was taken aback, then remembered how she and Harley's bird had hit it off.

"Don't mention that noisy little critter." Phoenix wrinkled her nose.

"I owe Harley a call. I'll tell him you sent your greetings. Parker is okay, and so is Harley by the way."

"Tell Harley that everything is going to turn out just fine, but it will take a while," Aunt Phoenix chipped in.

"Tell him we've got his back," added Celestine.

Harley was blessed to have a crew of kindly women of a certain age committed to his well-being and happiness. The ladies in the Aging Readers Club rooted for him on a regular basis and apparently two more guardians had joined the choir. Somewhere in heaven his mother must have had a hand in it, and he would need all the hands he could get as he went through Anna's belongings.

"Two things, before you go," Phoenix said as I finished my tea. "Grab a bunch of that basil running amuck in my garden. Do *not* forget to wear the charm when you see that man."

My aunt's telling use of the word *when* rather than *if* reminded me she often knew my mind before I knew it myself. For better or worse, simple coincidence had brought Terrence Davis back into my life. As my aunt observed, there was no such thing as happenstance, and years of her unflappable wisdom told me she was undoubtedly right.

Chapter 11

I slipped my mother's amulet around my neck before I left the house; call it heeding eccentric aunts or acknowledging Friday the thirteenth, it seemed the prudent thing to do. I was filled with dread, curiosity, and excitement, an unbalancing brew if ever there was one. I was eager to know what Terrence would say yet dreaded being pulled into the past. I also wanted to find out how long he had been living in Grovesville, and why I'd never run into him (and how to avoid running into him again). I dressed casually, maybe overly so, and offered to bring dessert, wine, or an appetizer. He said he didn't eat sweets or drink alcohol and for me to just bring myself, so I took him at his word.

I was surprised by his address. He'd alluded to the fact that he owned several buildings, and I assumed he lived in either Bren Bridge or a tony section of town, but his home was in a once fashionable section of Grovesville in which aging historic houses had been torn down and replaced by contemporary ones. The area was an interesting collection of bungalows, ranches, and bi-levels built in various decades. In many cases, the land itself was more valuable than the structure upon which it stood. Terrence's split-level had been built in the seventies, and I'd recently sold one with similar characteristics. The entryway stairs usually led to a comparatively small kitchen, open living/dining space, then continued up to three or four modest bedrooms.

Unsurprisingly, this one had been completely renovated. I suspected the contemporary touches had been initiated by his interior-decorating daughter. From my car, I could see that the attached garage had been greatly expanded to house at least three cars. I suspected that stairs from the garage led to the small landing that served as an entryway foyer to the rest of the house. In keeping with fashionable design, Rosalie had probably painted all the rooms—from kitchen to bedrooms—some muted natural shade of white and beige with skylights and floor-length windows bathing the place in sunlight during the day.

I sat in my car for longer than necessary before heading to the front door to ring the doorbell. The footsteps coming down the stairs to the foyer were surprisingly spry, and I muttered a silent curse. I'd assumed his daughter lived in the apartment above her salon, but I must have been wrong. He hadn't mentioned Rosalie's presence at dinner, and after her performance on Monday I wasn't looking forward to seeing her again. I gave my mother's blue lace agate a squeeze, pasted what I hoped was a convincing grin on my face, and prepared for whatever lay ahead. I was in for a pleasant surprise.

"Lord, it's been a long time, girl, too damn long!" said Jana Mae Jenkins.

No phony smile needed here. I burst into boisterous laughter. "Jana Mae! I am glad to see you. How have you been?" She was a plump, friendly woman who hugged with all her heart and might. When she pulled you into her warmth, she made you feel like a lost scared kid who'd just been found. Jana Mae and her husband, Robert, were much older than me and Darryl and were a husband and wife catering team just like us. We had become good friends and worthy competitors. After Darryl died, I'd allowed them and many of our mutual friends to slip from my life.

Jana Mae gave me another hug for good measure, then stood back to look me over. "We've missed you, honey, to say nothing of how much we do your precious husband."

"I know," I said. "I found it hard to reach out to people."

She nodded with a long sigh as if she understood. "So many people loved you both. It's time now to reach out again if you can; you've got to promise me you will. Robert is going to be mad that he missed seeing you, I'll tell you that!"

"I promise I'll be back in touch with you both, and everybody," I added with a pang of guilt.

"If you're not, then you'll be hearing from me. What are you doing here anyway? You're not after my job, are you?" she said, with what sounded like a cackle accompanied with a twinkle in her eye. "That's okay. If I have to lose this gig to somebody, better you than some fancy chef I don't know."

"Gig?" I was as puzzled by her question as much as her presence.

"Job. Girl, I'm a private chef!" She looked me up and down and then added with a wry smile, "Can't blame the man, though, for wanting someone easier on the eye. You are looking good!"

"No, I'm—"

"Don't tell me you're the guest!" She gave a chortle of a laugh. "Nice to be cooking for you, no matter who else is at the table. But you're a little early, honey. Mr. Davis won't be coming down for at least another ten minutes. He's not well, you know," she said, lowering her voice.

"You are Terrence's personal chef?" I still didn't get it.

She shrugged, "More or less, and for special occasions like when his daughter is coming over or has a client she wants to impress. I usually cook enough for a few days, shop for groceries, that kind of thing. He's picky about when and what he eats, won't eat sweets or fat, but he's going all out tonight, I'll tell you that." A timer went off in the kitchen, a sound we both knew well. "Come on up; let's catch up before he comes down."

The living area was as elegant as I suspected it would be and placed far enough from the kitchen for a person to fry fish and not have to smell it. The dining room table had been set up with silver and linen meant to impress, which made me uncomfortable.

"You did the table, right?"

"On his strict orders. You know, men don't know nothing about setting a table."

"Did he tell you anything about me?" I settled down on a wicker stool at the kitchen island across from the stove.

"No. None of my business, but he's a man with simple taste and the menu he requested tonight was a fancy one. Filet mignon with all the fixin's. Where do you know this guy from? Before Darryl, or did you just meet him?"

"Years before Darryl. Decades."

"You must have left quite an impression. He told me to get the best cut of beef I could get."

"Haven't eaten steak in years. A complete waste of money," I said with a touch of disdain, feeling sorry for Jana Mae, her work, and I was sure what would be an impressive presentation. Terrence Davis was holding on to a past that was long gone.

"I'll tell you one thing: This guy has money to burn," whispered Jana, leaning close. "And another thing, his daughter looks like a princess, but she's as fierce as a pit bull prepping for a fight, and I'd bet my money on her instead of the hound. She's a piece of work, though. Look out for that one if you're planning some kind of future with him. Guards her daddy something fierce."

"That's not going to happen. But does she live here?"

"No, in some fancy place in Bren Bridge, something he owns no doubt. But she's always here in his business. Opening mail, reading letters, bank statements, basically handles all his affairs, and he's got a lot of them because he owns a lot of property."

"How does he make his money?"

"Real estate and the market. He's good with investments, that's what I've heard anyway, and then there's his art and other stuff he collects." She nodded toward the upstairs bedrooms. "All those rooms are filled with artwork, old books, all kept a certain temperature, no sunlight, would you believe that? That garage downstairs? A couple of fancy cars in there, antiques I guess. She was here this morning cussing out the locksmith about the lock on the garage door being broken. I wouldn't want to cross her. Where do you know this guy from?" she asked, with a touch of nosiness.

The sound of Terrence coming downstairs stopped me from saying anything else and we quickly slipped into our roles: professional chef and expected guest. Jana Mae made a show of ushering me into the living room, then dashed back into the kitchen to plate our meals. I settled down on the cream-colored leather sofa, soft as a glove. I heard her say a few words to Terrence about warming up the food and returning in the morning to clean everything up; then she silently disappeared as good chefs are trained to do. I picked up a copy of *Art in America* lying on the coffee table and furiously leafed through it.

"Odessa, thank you for coming." Terrence sat down on the matching recliner across from me when he came into the room. I put the magazine back down on the table and quickly got to the point.

"You told me you wanted to explain what happened between us, and I want to hear what you have to say. But the truth is, we don't have much else to talk about." I regretted how callous my words sounded, but there was no sense in polite lies.

He looked stunned for a moment but quickly recovered. "I remember you always loved a good steak and—"

"I lost my taste for steak many years ago."

"Did it have something to do with me?"

"No," I said, but the truth was steaks reminded me of him and after things went bad the sight of one would turn my stomach. So there was a place for polite lies after all.

"What about dinner? Aren't you hungry?"

"No."

His face dropped. "I'm sorry if—"

"It's okay, really," I said. Dinner had been his idea, not mine, and I'd agreed to it without considering all it meant. I realized now that was a mistake. Better to have met somewhere for coffee, since he didn't drink, or come back to the studio on a day his daughter wouldn't be there. Despite the awkwardness that was now between us, I was still curious about what had happened; like the mysteries of the gift and the vagaries of my family, this was something I needed to understand.

"I'd like to start from the beginning," he said.

"No, just from when you didn't show up." I didn't feel like a recitation of his life story. Yet the anger and humiliation I'd felt about those days had begun to bubble inside. Thoughts of the vicious skills of my distant cousins suddenly spun through my head, and the futile wish that I'd possessed them during those devastating days. Instead, I'd simply waited for him to call or come, prayed for it, convinced until the very morning of our wedding that he would show up and I'd forgive him and we'd live happily ever after and life would turn out as we'd planned it.

"Why is my understanding of what happened then so important now?" I asked, although I knew the reason; he'd told me in the studio.

"I've never loved anyone as much as I did you, not then or now, and I owe you an explanation. Everything was closing in on me. I felt like I didn't have a choice. I was too ashamed to face you or my grandmother or your family."

"It was the week before our wedding." I hadn't meant my voice to quiver like it did, sounding nearly as hurt as it had all those years ago, but the hurt was lodged inside and found its way out. He dropped his head, shame still there, couldn't look me in the eye.

"The whole time I was with you I was lying, constantly, telling half-truths to cover what was going on. I was going down to Philly on trips I didn't need to make, making promises to her like I did to you."

"Her?" I was surprised by the stab of pain that shot through me.

"She was the kind of woman my grandmother hated, stubborn, impetuous, a touch crazy like my mother had been before the crack. That was the eighties, and that was what killed her, why Grandma had to raise me by herself. Maybe I needed a broken woman like my mother to make me feel whole. I still don't understand why I did it. I broke my grandmother's heart, the same way my mother did."

"You were involved with her the whole time we were together?"

"And before."

"What was her name?"

"Lil."

"What was she like?"

"She fancied herself a writer, wrote poetry, read all the time. She was bright and funny, despite her problems."

"And you loved her?"

"No, I despised her."

His puzzling words had to settle inside before I asked the obvious question. "Why?"

He took a breath, long and deep. "I knew she was pregnant, but she promised she had gotten rid of it. I gave her the money that she needed. The week before we were getting married I get a call from her at the hospital, saying I'd better come there and pick up what she'd left me. I didn't know what the hell she was talking about. I knew she was mad because I'd told her I was marrying you and I was breaking it off with her. I thought she understood, that it was settled and over between us."

He shook his head as if he were just getting the news and still couldn't believe it. "I get there, and they tell me the mother had split, naming me as the father, and that I had to take the baby with me or she'd go into foster care. I couldn't abandon her like my father had me. I wasn't going to do that to a kid. The next week was a blur of craziness—a paternity test to establish I was Rosalie's father, social services, getting ready to take her home to my grandmother because there was nowhere else to go. There was a note pinned to this cheap pink blanket; Lil had printed the words 'Rosa Lee. This one's for you!' on a page that looked like it was ripped from a notebook, something she just thought up out of spite, spur of the moment. I figured it meant 'here's my payback, one for you, a baby to take care of, a burden to be saddled with.' Took her back to my grandma's house. Didn't know what else to do."

"That must have shocked the heck out of your grandmother!" Evelyn Davis, prim and proper, came to mind.

"The minute she held Rosalie I knew everything would be okay. I wanted to name the baby Evelyn, after her, but she told me to keep the name her mother gave her. That it would be important to her someday, but I didn't want anything from her to touch my daughter. I just changed the spelling of her name from the ridiculous way her mother spelled it."

"Did you hear anything else from Lil?"

He shook his head. "Nothing."

"Your grandmother knew what happened?" I didn't try to hide my sense of betrayal.

"Don't blame her. I promised I'd tell you, but I couldn't bring myself to do it. You were so fragile then."

"I've never been that fragile in my life. Don't use that as an excuse," I snapped.

"No. I was just a coward."

"That sounds about right." I felt a mix of anger, sadness, disgust, and a surge of amusement as I recalled Aunt Phoenix's comments about this weak man and his weak chin.

"You should have told me."

"I know that now." He sighed before continuing. "My grandmother died six months after we moved in. Until the day she died, she assumed I'd told you and made things right. She'd wanted to call you herself, but I discouraged her, for obvious reasons. Told her to give you some space, trying to give myself some space to find a way to tell you."

"I'm sorry you didn't find that space. I liked and respected Miss Evelyn, and I would like to have spoken to her before she passed on, maybe found a way to keep her in my life for the short time she had left."

He kept any thoughts he had about what I'd said to himself. "It was a long time ago," he finally said, his voice low and tense. "I sold her house and we left Philly. There was nothing to keep us there. Grandma was as good an investor as she was a collector and left more than enough money to give me options. I went to Chicago, finished my MBA, got offers from several firms, lived in different cities and then abroad. When Rosalie got old enough I put her in a boarding school. I was making enough money for that."

"Sounds like you've had a pretty good life." I could think of nothing else to say.

"Not so much. And you?"

I managed a slight smile. "A very good one." I had no intention of sharing Darryl, our happiness, or my devastation at his loss. My memories were too precious to share with him. "How did you end up here?" I said, filling an uneasy silence.

"I got sick two years ago. Rosalie wanted to start a business and I was told there were good deals here, so I bought property, that building for her, this place for me. She renovated it, with the climate control rooms, place for the cars I'd begun to collect. I've become a collector these days, picking up anything and everything that strikes my fancy. This place is too big for me, but I needed the space for all my things."

He seemed tired again, his eyes wearier than before. Sharing his story had taken its toll on him, just as listening to it had on me, and I was eager now to leave. "Terrence, I can see how tired you are. It's time for me to go."

"But you came for dinner and everything is all ready, and I—"

"Another time when you're feeling better," I said, knowing that time would never come.

He nodded, obviously exhausted, then added, as if just remembering it, "There's one thing that haunts me every now and then. Before my grandmother died she mentioned she had a friend, an ob-gyn, who complained about some trifling woman—as she put it—abandoning a baby. Grandma didn't think much about it at the time, but wondered later if it could have been Lil, and if that note she left me meant she had taken one baby and left one for me. It would be like Lil to do something callous like that, to have the last damn word."

"Did you check with the hospital?"

"They wouldn't tell me anything. We weren't related and I had no right to any of her records. I finally did some research on my own through one of those sites where you look for family, even put in a DNA sample, but never heard anything back. But I'd changed addresses so many times I . . ." His voice faded with that last thought. "Too late for that now. Rosalie is my heart. My only child, and I've committed my life to her. Even if somebody reached out it wouldn't be worth the trouble at this point. I'm dying and there's nothing I could do. I just need to be comfortable, that's all, and Rosalie sees to that."

"Terrence, it really is time to let the past go, all of it, and enjoy what you have with your daughter. I'll give her a call and let her know I had to leave early, so she can come by, and eat that delicious-looking steak!" I added, trying to leave on a light note.

"Thanks, Odessa."

I waited until he made his way upstairs, each step taking more out of him than the last, before I left.

I considered dropping by Lennox Royal's place on the way home not so much for food as company, someone to share this evening with to put it in its proper place, but halfway there I realized I was talked out and nearly as exhausted as Terrence. I left the promised message for Rosalie, doctored up a can of tomato soup with diced tomatoes, heavy cream, and some of Aunt Phoenix's basil leaves, and threw together a grilled cheese sandwich with sharp cheddar and creamery butter. A text from Lennox flashed on my phone asking me to call when I could, but I wasn't up to carrying on a conversation. That upturned stone had taken more out of me than I ever imagined it could. Juniper was the only sentient being whose company I needed.

Chapter 12

It promised to be a lazy Saturday, the best kind and just what I needed. I was still shaken by my time with Terrence and couldn't get him or the things he'd told me out of my mind. The past was gone forever, yet he was still haunted by it, and I felt sorry for him. I thought about calling later to check on him, then changed my mind. I'd found out what I wanted to know, and there was no reason to reach out and get pulled back into our shared history.

I took my own good time getting out of bed, getting dressed, then slipping on my mother's amulet out of a sense of guilty duty. After feeding Juniper, I treated myself to a fat-laden breakfast: buttered toast, cream in my coffee, omelet made with leftover cheddar cheese. I texted Lennox, then called Louella, who didn't answer, which didn't surprise me. I left a message saying I was worried about her, we needed to talk and hoped to see her Monday at work.

I'd put Aunt Phoenix's basil in a jar of water when I got home Monday night, but it was wilting fast and screaming *pesto!* Luckily, there were pine nuts in my freezer, a block of Parmesan cheese in the fridge, and that, along with virgin olive oil and garlic, meant I could return Aunt Phoenix's gift in a different form with enough left over to surprise Vinton, who also loved pesto.

Cooking, even something as simple as this sauce, always sends my mind on a winding journey as calming as meditation. Pesto was as easy to make as puttanesca without the colorful history, and that brought back my evening with Bella, bringing a smile, then a sigh when recalling what she'd told me about Anna's past. I ground the pine nuts in the processor, slowly added olive oil, then garlic, and pulsed until they were smooth. I chopped up the basil, picking up a bunch to inhale, its unmistakable fragrance bringing back Darryl and the basil, tomatoes, and zucchini we'd buy at a nearby farmer's market. Sipping wine on a deck meant summer to some folks, but for me and my husband it had been fresh basil and farm-grown tomatoes and the promise each year that we'd remember to plant them.

I allowed myself to dwell in that memory for some moments as I pulsed the leaves with the pine nuts, garlic, and olive oil, which reminded me of the green in the unmatched outfits of my two quarrelsome aunts, and that made me laugh. I was grating Parmesan cheese, telling myself it was time to buy it grated like most people, when the doorbell rang. Twice, then three times. Puzzled, then annoyed, I went to answer it. I was stunned when I saw who was standing there.

"Good morning. Do you mind if I come in for a moment?" said Rosalie Davis in her well-mannered voice.

"No, of course not," I said too quickly, and led her into the living room, offering her a seat on the confessional couch, wondering if its magic could break her formality. I was sure Rosalie's visit had something to do with her father and what he had said at our dinner that wasn't one. I wondered how much more she knew about our past. Before sitting down, she

looked around the room with the critical glance of a professional decorator, then nestled her thin, neat body into one of
the soft gray easy chairs in front of the fireplace. I sat next to
her in the other.

"This room has beautiful bones; when you decide to do
something with it, like redecorating or resetting, I'd love to
give you some advice."

"Thank you but no thanks. I'm very pleased with the way
it looks," I said, defensively. "I have many good memories
here," I added, softening my tone.

"Good memories are great if you have them," she said,
hinting that she didn't have many, which made me wonder
about the life she'd led with her father. He'd talked mostly
about himself last night, sharing little about his daughter.

"Before I forget, thank you for calling me to tell me what
was going on with my dad. We both appreciated that."

"Glad I could help. How is he doing? He wasn't—"

"He asked me to give you this," she said, cutting me off as
she reached into her black leather tote bag and took out a
book. It was a well-worn copy of *I Know Why the Caged Bird
Sings*. "First edition, signed. He wanted you to have it," she
said, handing it to me.

"I don't know what to say—"

"He wanted you to have it," she repeated.

"I love Maya Angelou, and she is my aunt's favorite writer."
Terrence must have forgotten that it was Aunt Phoenix, not
me, who collected her books. At least I knew what I'd be giving my aunt for Christmas next year. "Thank you."

"Thank him."

We sat there for a few moments, me skimming through a
book I'd read many times before, Rosalie staring at the fireplace as if a fire were burning in the grate. I was puzzled by
her preoccupation with the empty fireplace, and in the back
of my mind I was worried about the whereabouts of Juniper,

who never missed a visitor. I'd left that pesto uncovered on the kitchen counter, and although he wasn't a vegetarian by any stretch of the imagination, I'd seen him gleefully chomp down on a wedge of Brie.

"I certainly appreciate your coming by," I said, risking rudeness and preparing to go to the kitchen to check. "I'll certainly give your father a call." I wasn't sure if she heard me; she seemed firmly planted in her chair.

"Please don't go." She suddenly looked up, begging me to stay.

"Sure, of course. But let me get you something to drink, some coffee or tea?" I noticed again the peculiar glimmer I'd seen when I met her. It was an unusual one, shifting from color to color so quickly they were hard to distinguish. What did this say about her, if anything?

"Can I ask you something?" Her question pulled me back to her face from the colors shifting around her.

"Yes, but before we talk, could I ask you something first?" Her glimmer had brought back the puzzling ones of the Delbartons, the bronze hue that surrounded Emily and Edgar's ghoulish green.

"About what?" she said, her tone wary.

"Just about work, that's all."

"Work? Sure. What about it?"

"Do you know the Delbartons well? Your father mentioned he'd bought some property from them."

"Not really, she was my boss; why do you ask?"

"What do you think about Edgar?"

A slight, puzzling smile crossed her lips. "He was obsessed with Anna Lee. I know that. When she died I thought maybe he had something to do with it. I was going to tell the police, but then I changed my mind. It was just a hunch, and I didn't want to cause any trouble with the Delbartons."

"Maybe you should tell them."

"It's odd that you should mention them. Emily recently called me about a job, and before she hung up told me to call her right away if I saw or heard from her brother because she was worried about him."

"She didn't say why?"

"No, but she sounded desperate, something that Emily Delbarton never sounds."

"What is your take on Edgar, her brother? I've heard that he's a little off. What do you think?"

She shrugged. "There are those who say the whole family is a little bit off. I just avoided him when I worked there."

"You knew Anna Lee from there?"

She looked surprised. "Yeah, more or less. Where do you know my father from? He said he knew you from a long time ago. From how long ago? Did you know my mother?" She asked the questions quickly, not giving me a chance to answer.

"Your father and I were engaged once, before you were born, and we broke up. A very long time ago." I made it simple.

"You didn't know my mother?" She was longing for an answer I couldn't give; it was in her eyes.

"Never met her. What did your father tell you about her?" I kept my voice neutral.

She shook her head. "Not much. He called her Lil, said her name was Lily; when I contacted the hospital where I was born they said she spelled it strange, not like most people do. That was all they would tell me about her."

"Does your father know that you contacted the hospital?"

"I try to keep things from him that will disturb him. I don't want him to worry himself. That's why I take care of everything. Everything."

"You're a good daughter."

"I'm the only real family he has; it's as simple as that," she said with a heartbreaking sadness. "He took care of me, and now it's my turn to take care of him."

"Your father mentioned that the two of you traveled quite a bit when you were a child. What interesting places did you go?" I said, trying to lighten our conversation.

"He sent me to boarding schools in Europe and the states when I was growing up. Sometimes I have a hard time connecting to people. Most of the time it doesn't matter much," she said, not the answer I was hoping for.

She seemed uneasy and stood abruptly, ready to leave. The distance she felt around others had suddenly become apparent. I felt sorry for her discomfort but was more worried about Juniper. I glanced toward the kitchen hoping he hadn't made his way to the pesto. Suddenly she changed her mind, sat back down, her gaze drawn to my amulet.

"Can I see it?" she asked. I took it off and handed it to her.

"It's beautiful, but it's very heavy." She examined it and gave it back. "It's a blue lace agate, a gift from my mother. Even though it weighs me down, I wear it because of that," I said, placing it back around my neck.

"My mother gave me something, too; that's what my father told me. *Rosalie*. She gave me my name. Not as heavy as your stone, though. I wear it lightly," she said with an odd girlish giggle.

"It's something she must have wanted you to have."

"Are they having some kind of memorial or something for Anna Lee? I want to go and contribute, like money," she said as if the thought had just occurred to her. It took me by surprise.

I answered cautiously, startled by her interest. "The police are still searching for next of kin. She left some personal papers with a friend who is going through them to see what can be found."

"Friend? What friend?"

The urgency in her voice surprised me, and she didn't wait for me to tell her.

"Papers? Could you tell me who her friends are so I can call them and check about the memorial? Can you tell me their e-mails or something, their phone numbers so I can text?" I was unsure about telling her anything, and she was too anxious to wait for my answer. "I know there was Bella, and that other girl who was with you at the party and her boyfriend, Harry."

"Harley."

"Well, I just want to help out you know, in any way I can. I'd like to be in touch with them, whoever will be able to tell me something."

"I'll call you as soon as we decide what to do," I said.

"Don't forget, okay? I need to pay my respects."

"I won't. I'll also give your father a call to thank him for the book."

"Don't bother. I'll tell him for you. He finds things disturbing these days and I need to look out for him."

"Understood," I said, puzzled by her reluctance. "I'll leave it up to you then,"

"We are a team, my father and me. We always have been. I look out for him and he looks out for me," she said, repeating nearly verbatim what she'd said before, which made me wonder why. "Thank you for talking to me and for the information." Her smile was brief and amiable.

"Your father is lucky to have you," I said, and meant it. She gave a curt nod, as if in agreement, then avoided my eyes when she closed the door.

"Well, that was certainly interesting," I said to Juniper, when he finally made his way downstairs. "I think that girl is actually scared that there might still be something between me and her father. Maybe I should have told her the truth. What do you think?" He answered with a loud meow. "That ship sailed before it launched," I said, chuckling at the thought of it as I filled his bowl with food. "Thank you for not getting into my pesto." Rosalie's visit had indeed been "interesting," as I'd told my furry companion yet it had left me uneasy, and I wasn't sure why.

Chapter 13

The week started off badly and got worse by the day. By Friday night, all I wanted to do was sip (gulp) merlot, gorge myself on leftover chocolate chips, and crawl into bed. My downward spiral began Monday before I woke up when Louella, apparently rising with the birds, delivered a disturbing early-morning call.

"I needed to talk before you left for work, while everybody is still asleep," she whispered into the phone, troubling in itself.

"Can't we talk at work? I'll take you out to lunch; how about that?" I mumbled, not yet awake.

"No. I'm not coming in this week. The car is still in the shop, and I don't want to take the bus again."

"What happened to the car?" I opened my eyes.

"Red hit something. I told you that. Maybe I didn't; I don't know! I've just been in a, well, a really bad state."

"What did he hit?" I asked, fully awake.

"I've got to find some balance, Dessa. Decide what to do about my life. I don't want Erika or Red to hear anything I'm going to tell you. Or anybody else for that matter, except you. Nobody," she said without answering my question.

"What kind of conversation are we talking about?" I said, sitting up straight.

"A very private one. I know how you worry about me, how you promised my mom you'd look out for me. I need to talk to you before I make this life-changing decision one way or the other. I need your help in making it."

"Life-changing decision?"

"Yeah. It might ruin everybody's life. Mine, Red's, and most of all Erika's. I never want to do to Erika what my mother did to me."

"Does this have something to do with Anna Lee?" I tossed out my biggest fear, the one that had haunted me since my visit to BUNS.

The line went silent; my heart dropped. "Louella? Are you there? You need to tell me what is going on!" I could hear a child whining in the background. Erika was up and trying to get her mother's attention.

"I can't talk now. I will when I can. I only called because I knew you were worried about me and I wanted to get back to you."

"I'm still worried about you! I'm going to come by tonight and you're going to tell me what the heck is going on!"

"No! Please wait. Please!"

"Then when? I need you to give me a date."

Another pause. "Can you come by this Sunday? Red is taking Erika to visit his mother, so we can talk then. Okay?"

"Sunday morning. I'll see you then. Don't forget, because I will be there bright and early."

"Thank you for being such a good friend, for trying to look after me like you told my mother you would." The line went dead, leaving me no chance to say anything else.

I couldn't get Louella's call out of my head. It played in my mind as I dressed for work, tended to Juniper's various needs, and packed up the pesto for Aunt Phoenix and Vinton, wishing too late that I'd made enough for myself. I decided to deliver my aunt's pesto on the way to work, which would give me a credible excuse to leave quickly without lingering to talk. I wasn't ready to share this weekend's events and knew my aunts would be eager to hear every sordid detail. In the meantime, I'd have to wait until Sunday to see Louella. It was a long wait, but the moment I saw her I'd know immediately what was going on in her life; the color of her glimmer would tell me. If it had grown deeper, nearer to that terrible shade it had been when I met her, I'd know she was in real trouble. If it had lightened, I'd know she was okay. I'd simply have to be patient and wait to find out.

I refused to let myself believe that Louella could have anything to do with Anna's death, yet a nagging notion kept edging itself into my thoughts, warning me that maybe I didn't know her as well as I thought. Despite my closeness to her mother, I'd had no sense that her life would take such a violent turn. Nor could I forget Lennox's belief that an apple never fell far from the tree and that there was always a devil within each of us just waiting to be poked. Louella had become like a younger sister to me, one of my blended family that Lennox regarded with a jaundiced eye.

And then there was Blade and his talk about some random woman who came to BUNS asking about Anna. He wasn't clear about the time line and he hadn't seen her himself, yet from the moment he told me I thought it might be Louella who had claimed Anna was not what she seemed to be. How did she know that? Yet those words could have simply been the envy of an insecure woman toward a charming newcomer who had effortlessly captured everyone's heart. Just what had Red hit with her car and why didn't she tell me? He was notoriously overprotective of Louella and Erika. Had she shared her feelings about Anna and that she felt threatened by her? Did he have some misguided impulse to protect her?

It seemed farfetched yet was bothersome enough to make me forget the amulet. I was halfway to my aunt's house when I remembered it and had to go back to get it. The last thing I needed was a shame-inducing lecture from my aunts. As usual, the front door was unlocked, and I walked in to find the two of them sitting at the kitchen table sipping coffee and nibbling chocolate croissants. Phoenix was methodically filling out the crossword puzzle from the Sunday paper—in ink. Celestine was reading the business section. Neither looked up when I entered the room.

"Brought you some pesto. Hope you enjoy it. Gotta run," I said, putting the pesto on the table between them and turning to go, which got their attention.

"Sit down for a minute." Celestine looked up with a smile.

"We've been worried about you and the chinless wonder all weekend. So tell us what happened?" Phoenix glanced up from her puzzle.

"Not much to talk about. We chatted a while, and I left." I tried to sound casual even though I assumed they probably knew I was lying. Aunt Phoenix didn't disappoint.

"Right," she said, scribbling a word into her puzzle.

"Don't worry, darling; we won't judge. You can tell us anything," said Celestine.

"Or not," said Phoenix, scowling at her sister. "She's a grown woman, Celestine; it's her business, not ours. She'll say what she has to say when she's ready to say it."

"On my way! Love you two! See you later. I've got houses to sell and contracts to write!" I said breezily, heading to the door for a quick getaway.

"Not so fast," said Aunt Phoenix, rising from her chair in time to grab my arm just before I made it. "Listen to me, Odessa. Do not take that amulet off, do you hear me? I know it's heavy, but keep it on until you see us again. Do you understand?"

I pulled away, stunned by the look in her eyes and concern in her voice. What did she know? Could it have something to do with Louella?

"Am I in danger?" I didn't bother to hide my distress.

"Just wear your mother's protective charm, that's all," said Celestine from the table.

"I mean you-all would tell me if I were, right?"

"We can only tell you what we know, and that is that you need to wear that charm until you see us again," said Phoenix in the no-nonsense voice I'd heard and feared since I was six.

"But what good is our gift if it can't tell you or me something as basic as that?" I said, pulling away from my aunt. "What good are all the glimmers, and annoying smells, crazy gray streaks, and occasional irrational glimpses into the future when you can't do anything about it!"

They glanced at each other, then back at me, and I realized with a start that they didn't have a clue.

"It certainly helps with the stock market," said Celestine, trying to reassure me. "A loser stock splits out of the blue, and you look up and say, 'Thank you, gift, for helping me out!'"

"Well, that's never happened to me," I grumbled.

"Like winning when you play the lottery when you actually play what's been suggested," added Phoenix with a subtle swipe at me for forgetting to play her numbers.

"When you're ready, we'll share essential things you need to know before we leave," said Celestine, bringing a mysterious nod from Phoenix.

"Are you talking about leaving Jersey or leaving for good?" Her ominous words made me wonder again about the rituals and secrets they kept to themselves.

Both shrugged as if on cue, leaving it up to me to guess.

"I don't want to know anytime soon," I said, alarmed by

her words. "Okay, I promise to wear the thing," I added, giving Aunt Phoenix the promise she needed along with a hug, which she returned more firmly than was needed.

"Now that that's settled, how about next Monday for dinner? Ask Harley and Parker if they'd like to come," said Celestine, half joking.

"I'll let you know," I said, closing *and* locking the front door behind me.

I found a parking space in front of Risko Realty, a rarity on any day, particularly on a Monday, and wondered if I owed "the gift" a thank-you. I touched the amulet on my way into the building, heavy as it was, and felt stronger with it around my neck. I knew it was the presence of my mother more than the stone itself. If there was magic it came from her.

The roses were the first thing I saw when I came in, standing on my desk regal and beautiful in their fancy cut-glass vase. I stopped dead at the sight of them, scared, angry, not sure what to do except scream, because there was no doubt where they came from.

"They were here for you and Bella this morning, leaning against the office door. I brought them inside before I realized who they were from," said Vinton, who came to stand behind me as if I might faint. "I put Bella's on the floor near the coffeemaker so I could take them out with the trash. I was going to put yours there, too; then I saw that note and figured you might want to read it."

"They're from Edgar Delbarton."

"I figured as much."

"Bella told me about him. Should we call the cops?"

"I don't know." I placed my tote bag and pocketbook next to the roses and dropped into my chair. "What would we say to them, that this guy sent roses and we want to report him?"

They were all the same deep red colors he'd sent Anna, and the smell of them turned my stomach. I opened the envelope and quickly read the card: "ANGEL. I WANT WHAT SHE LEFT ME" was written in caps. I remembered a line about angels in the poem Edgar was obsessed with but couldn't recall exactly what it was; a vague sense of wariness crept over me. Bella came in then, saw me, grinned, saw my flowers, screamed. Catching my eye, Vinton headed to the coffee table to get rid of those Edgar had left for her, but it was too late; she'd seen them.

"Those are for me, aren't they?" Her voice was trembling.

"Don't worry, Sweetie. I'm putting them outside in the trash in five minutes," Vinton said, picking up the bouquet to haul outside. "I'll be back for yours in a minute, Sunshine." Before he got to the door, I checked Bella's bouquet to see if there was a note attached and was relieved to see there was nothing.

Bella put her head in her hands and sank into the chair next to mine. "Why is he still doing this?"

I shook my head. "I don't know. He must still be obsessed with Anna, and we're mixed in with his obsession."

"Where does it end?"

"I'll tell you where it ends if he brings his skinny butt in here," said Vinton, returning for my bouquet. "I will give him a beatdown like he's never been beat down before!" After he'd left, we both managed a smile at Vinton's tough-guy swagger, despite the situation. At his age and in his physical condition administering a beatdown to anybody was out of the question.

"Don't worry. You both are going to be okay," he said when he returned to his cubicle.

"You're right," I said as I turned on my computer. "Like most bullies he's basically a coward. Remember how you scared him when he was here before." I nodded at Bella, reminding her of the bad-ass girl persona she'd pulled out of nowhere.

"Are you telling me he was actually in this office?" Vinton said, his voice rising in outrage. "Bella, you didn't tell me that!"

"I didn't want to worry you," she said sheepishly. "He basically turned tail and ran when I stood up to him."

"A beatdown Bella Mondavi style," I said, making my voice light, but Bella was scared now; that was clear. All color had drained from her face and she'd tucked her shoulders into her body as if protecting herself. I remembered his words from that night: "I will never give up. Never!" he'd said, and the fear in Bella's eyes told me she hadn't forgotten them either.

"We need to tell the queen," Vinton nodded toward Tanya's office. "Maybe she can hire some bodyguards or get a protective order against him or call Emily Delbarton and ask her to keep him on a leash."

"You know this is Tanya's week in Massachusetts," I reminded him.

"Massachusetts? What the heck is she doing in Massachusetts?" said Bella.

"Canyon Ranch. Spa treatments," said Vinton disdainfully. "How could I forget!"

"Even if she knew, I doubt Tanya would go up against Emily Delbarton. I'm not sure it would do much good one way or the other," I said, recalling what Rosalie had told me about Emily reaching out to her about her brother's whereabouts.

"Are we on our own?"

"Looks that way. But if he does come back he'll be trespassing and then we can call the police," I said, trying to reassure Bella.

"No, I'll kick his backside for scaring my ladies, and then we'll call the police," said Vinton, thrusting out his bony chest, which brought a furtive smile from Bella.

The good thing was, Edgar Delbarton didn't come back, depriving Vinton of his chance to display his street creds. Yet the flowers kept coming. Every day bringing a new bouquet, each one larger than the last, all in different shades of red. Crimson. Scarlet. Vermillion. Carmine. I never knew roses came in so many hues. There were no notes, nothing revealing the sender or the name of the florist. Nothing about angels or wanting what belonged to him. Just the flowers left sitting in front of Risko Realty, which Vinton immediately tossed into the trash.

"At some point, he'll stop wasting his money when he sees what's filling that dumpster in the alley," Vinton observed. I nodded as if I agreed but wasn't so sure.

"You never know what people not in their right minds are going to do. Even though he hasn't come in here, I don't feel safe. Can't we do something, tell the police that he's threatening us?" said Bella on Wednesday night. "I dread coming to work tomorrow."

"Not for flowers. He hasn't really done anything to us, just sent flowers," I explained calmly, but was as frustrated as she was. I didn't mention the strange note he'd written on the first delivery. It had been for me, and there was no need to put more of a scare into Bella.

"Tanya's name is on the business. When she comes back on Monday, we'll tell her that she has to hire a guard or call the cops or close the office. We can't do much on our own. We're not even sure who is sending them. There's no signature or anything. We'll just need to wait him out," said Vinton.

"But he's taunting us!" said Bella, close to crying.

"Sooner or later this is going to stop," I said, hoping to reassure her.

The next morning, it seemed that I was right. When Friday morning came and left with no roses, we took a collective breath of relief.

"I was scared I was going to have to quit," said Bella, relaxed and smiling for the first time this week.

"I was looking forward to proving I still had my chops," said Vinton. I said a silent thank-you to the gift and squeezed my mother's amulet.

I left the office feeling a weight had been lifted. That changed quickly when I drove into my driveway.

"Well, somebody certainly loves you!" my neighbor Julie called out as I parked my car. She was sitting on my front stairs waiting for me with a big wave and a bigger grin. "A delivery-man rang my bell and said he had something for you, but you weren't home. Guess he tried your bell first and didn't want to leave them on your porch."

"A delivery?" Dread swept me, an omen from the gift.

"Gorgeous red roses, deep black red. I looked it up. Red roses mean love forever, but it was kind of a weird bouquet, had a white chrysanthemum stuck right in the middle of it. Strange choice. Looked that up, too. Florist must have made a mistake."

"What kind of mistake?"

"A bad one. White mums mean death, not love. There's a card attached, too. Do you think it's from your chef ex-cop friend? If it's him, he should get himself a new florist or get his flowers straight. But what a sweet thing to do! I always loved getting flowers from a man, or from anybody for that matter, but there's something special—"

I didn't hear the rest. I couldn't have listened even if I'd tried. I sat down on her front step unsure if I could make it to her porch. One thought went through me: *He knows where I live. He knows how to reach me.*

"What did he look like, the guy who brought the flow-ers?" I cut into what had become her monologue.

"Funny you should ask. Rather an odd-looking chap for a deliverer of bouquets. Very dour, dressed in black, looked like he was headed for a funeral. I told him to wait for a tip, but he was gone before I came back."

"Where are they now?"

"The flowers? Took them inside the house. Come on in. I'm dying to know what that note says."

I followed Julie into her neat, safe house to where she had put them on her dining room table. They were the deepest red yet, almost maroon, the white chrysanthemum popping from the center delivering its own frightening message. The note was tied to a stem. I snatched it off and read it.

"What does it say?" Julie asked, not hiding her eagerness.

"It's—very personal." I avoided her eyes hoping she wouldn't see the panic that I knew was in my own. "I'd better get home now," I added as casually as I could, picking up the large bouquet, hauling it outside, down the sidewalk, and up my stairs. "Thank you for bringing it inside!" I yelled back at her.

"So nice to have someone thoughtful in your life!" she yelled back, sounding wistful, as I closed the door behind me.

I threw the flowers in a black garbage bag, tying it up as if they were alive. I tossed it on my back porch, keeping the note to read again, then ran upstairs, grabbed the book of Poe's poems, and tore through it, searching for "Annabel Lee." The first four lines were the same as in the poem, the last ones, the frightening ones, seemed to be written just for me:

> *Angel, you will not dissever my soul from hers.*
> *At night-tide I will lie down by her side.*
> *You will see. You will see. You will see me*
> *and my Annabel Lee. I will take what she has left me.*

Did Edgar Delbarton see me as the angel who had killed his love? Would he try to seek his revenge?

Harley had left a message earlier in the day, and when I listened to it now I understood what must have set Edgar off. Anna had been killed nearly a month ago on a Saturday.

Harley said he was having a hard time dealing with that anniversary but had marked it with going through the rest of her things. He had found something he needed to share with me and wanted me to call him when I could. I was in no shape to call him and offer comfort tonight; it was all I could do to comfort myself.

I called Lennox Royal at midnight. He'd told me to reach out if I ever felt threatened, and that was now. I left a message saying I had clients in the afternoon, but I'd drop by his place at closing so we could talk. And finally, around 4:00 in the morning, I fell into a broken, fearful sleep.

Chapter 14

I got to Lennox's place as he was closing up. Food was packed away, Georgia had left, and a lonesome diner had politely been asked to leave. Lennox took one look at me and sat me down at the counter, coming back in five minutes with a jar of clover honey and pot of chamomile tea. Over the next fifteen minutes, I told him everything that had happened since Anna Lee's death—beginning and ending with those dreadful roses.

"This tea is good for nerves, but after hearing what you just told me, you may need something stronger." He settled down across from me on the stool he keeps behind the counter. "What do you know about this Edward Delbarton guy?"

"Edgar. He's the younger brother of Emily Delbarton from that rich family that owns Delbarton Estates—"

"I know who they are." Lennox's raised eyebrow indicated he knew more than he was willing to say. "Emily's diamond-ringed fingers are known to stir a bunch of nasty pots."

"You must be talking about BUNS."

He looked startled, then shook his head as if surprised.

"How did you find that out? That's just the tip, but it's not common knowledge."

"Anna worked at BUNS before Risko Realty. That's where Edgar Delbarton met her."

"Your young lady got around," he said with a slender smile.

"Yeah, I'm afraid she did. Ever heard of a guy name Blade?"

"Blade? On occasion." A scowl said it was all he was going to say. I tried again anyway.

"Is he trustworthy?"

He smiled, amused that I was going for more than he intended to give. "On occasion. What did Blade have to say?"

"That Emily Delbarton owned the club, that Anna was a nice girl who maybe knew more than she should."

"How did you find all that out?"

"You don't want to know," I said, and meant it.

Lennox's frown told me I was glimpsing the serious detective that he kept hidden. "Okay, I'll let that ride, but that dangerous relationship might explain the roses. They could be a warning to you or anybody who she may have shared things with to keep their mouths closed. You know you need to be careful, right, Odessa?"

"I know, but the roses were definitely from Edgar, not Emily. When I thanked her for sending them her face went blank. She had no idea what I was talking about."

He paused and took a lengthy sip of tea. "Let's go in a different direction. Who else would be angry or jealous enough to want this young woman dead?"

I sipped my tea, added honey, focused hard on the stirring of my spoon. Good detective that he was, he saw through me.

"Okay, Odessa. Who else? Let me guess. Somebody you don't want to believe could do it but can't get that possibility out of your mind, right? That's called a hunch; sometimes they're good, sometimes plain dumb, but you do need to acknowledge them."

"Blade mentioned a young woman who came to the club looking for Anna. But he didn't see her himself, so he couldn't describe her, and—"

"You're afraid that mysterious woman is that apple who didn't fall far from her tree, right? Would this apple have a motive, wrecked car, history with the victim?"

"Not really," I said too quickly, wondering if two out of three made Louella a possible suspect.

"There's an old saying that murder is committed for one of four reasons, all beginning with *l*: loot, loathing, lust, love."

"Edgar fills two. Lust and love," I said, eager to offer him up.

"Those are powerful motives, no doubt about that." Lennox nodded in agreement. "What did you do with the note that came with the flowers? Maybe it can tell us something."

"Tore it up, threw it away, didn't want to look at it again."

"Okay." His mildly critical glance said it wasn't the wisest thing to do. "Can you remember what it said, particularly the last few sentences?"

I told him word for word because I couldn't get them out of my mind:

> " '*Angel, you will not dissever my soul from hers.*
> *At night-tide I will lie down by her side.*
> *You will see. You will see. You will see me*
> *and my Annabel Lee. I will take what she has left me.*' "

"He's referring to you as 'Angel'?"

"I guess so."

"Why did he think she left something for him with you?"

"Heck if I know, but it scares the mess out of me."

"What about that night-tide stuff about lying down by her side? What do you think he means by that?'

"Anna was killed on a Saturday night almost a month ago. Maybe he's trying to tell me something he wants me to know about her. His note said: 'You will see me and my Annabel Lee. I know now what she left me.'"

"Any idea what he's talking about?"

"No, but I think I need to go back to where they found her; maybe he'll be looking for what he imagines she left him."

"You're kidding me, right?" Lennox leaned back on his stool, eyes widening in disbelief.

"I just want to go back there, Lennox. Maybe there are answers that can put an end to all this. To Harley's grief, to everything. If I just drive by, see if I missed something, see what I can—"

"Something you missed? The cops have gone through that place. It's still considered a crime scene. There's nothing there that hasn't been seen and examined. There is no evidence. Come on, Dessa." His tone was kindly yet firm, the same one he'd used with the reluctant diner when it was time to go home.

I considered for a moment (a very brief one) sharing that secret part of myself that could see and understand things cops would never grasp. I would know exactly what he meant by night-tide lying down by her side. Maybe Emily or her associates did have something to do with Anna's death. Maybe those roses meant that he was trying to warn me to beware of her. He had tried to protect Anna when he got her away from BUNS; maybe he was leaving a message for me now. Did I have everything wrong? Was the Angel who had "dissevered" his soul from hers Emily, not me? If I visited the space where she died, only then would I understand what he was talking about.

"You will forgive me for asking this, I know you are an independent tough woman and all, but I have too much self-respect to let you go out there by yourself. If something happened to you, I'd never forgive myself. I can't take that kind of guilt at this point in my life. If you insist upon going, please let me drive out there with you."

"But this is my problem, not yours."

"Come on, you know me better than that."

"It's probably a good idea," I said; the truth was that I knew he was right.

"Thank you," he said as though he meant it.

Whenever Lennox and I met for dinners or lunches, we arrived and left in separate cars, always parking on the street and meeting at the restaurant. This was the first time I'd been a passenger in his car; it was an intimacy that took getting used to. I wasn't prepared for this cherry-red Mercedes, the same color and model as Tanya Risko's, that he led me to. The man and the car didn't fit, yet I had to admit it was a pleasant sensation climbing in when he opened the door—a far cry from squeezing into my cramped, occasionally smelly Subaru.

"Wow!" I muttered as I settled into the interior as plush and soft as velvet.

"Don't get excited. Ain't mine. Belongs to my ex-wife, and comes with Lena for the weekend. Lena loves it, so here it is."

"I don't blame her; it's a beautiful car," I said, touching the various knobs and dials with a kid's curiosity. "Smells good, too," I added as I breathed in the subtle scent of lemon floating in from an unseen source.

Lennox rolled down the window with a vengeance. "Well, you're welcome to it. It's used, what do they call it, pre-owned. I'll take my Honda any day of the week."

"You can have your Honda, but this does make one feel

elegant," I said, gazing up at the darkening sky through the sunroof.

"My ex-wife is the kind of woman who always demanded elegance and perfection, no matter the price, not an easy thing to maintain on a detective's salary unless you cross over to the other side," he said with a bitterness I'd never heard before.

"Other side?"

"That's what I said."

"How long were you two married?" I couldn't help but ask.

"Too long," he muttered.

"Well, this is a nice car," I said, agreeably.

"The truth is, though, there is nothing as expensive as a used Mercedes. Something is always broken, and she spends a ton of money because she likes the way it looks."

"Each to her own." I tried to lighten the conversation. The mention of his ex-wife had clearly darkened Lennox's mood.

"You're right." He forced a smile. "A couple of days ago, I saw a Benz older than this one. I think it was a 300 SEL. I know the model because a gangster I arrested in the old days drove one. It was big, fancy, and cost somebody a fortune to maintain if it was driven at all. You could definitely call that one elegant. Probably made in the 1970s; these days that would probably be considered vintage."

My thoughts turned to Terrence at the mention of antiques and then to Friday's visit, which brought an involuntary sigh, louder than I meant it to be.

"I don't guess a penny or dollar will buy what brought that sigh on, will it?" Lennox asked with a sideways glance.

"I was thinking about an old friend, a love actually, who came into my life recently, and that thought of him makes me sad."

"So it ended badly?"

"Well, he left me at the altar," I said with a self-conscious chuckle.

"Left you at the altar! Thank God you didn't marry him! What kind of fool leaves a woman as special as you at the altar or anywhere else? You're not letting him back into your life, are you?" Lennox, not bothering to hide his outrage, gave me an anxious, concerned look.

"No, he's very sick, and dying, and that's what that sigh was about. But he's luckier than a lot of people. He has a daughter who is extremely protective. She's kind of overbearing but looks out for him. It's as if they've reversed roles."

"He's lucky to have her." Lennox's sudden change of expression revealed an emotion he may not have wanted me to see.

"What's wrong, Lennox?" I took a chance he'd tell me, and to my surprise he did.

"What you were saying reminds me of my situation and makes me worry about Lena and me. I have to be there for her in a way that she can never be there for me and that haunts me. She will never be able to fully take care of herself and that is scary as hell. Keeps me up at night, if you want to know the truth."

"But she has two parents." I asked after a beat, "What about her mother?"

He snorted, shook his head in disgust. "Like I said, my ex-wife is a woman who demands perfection, in all things. Lena is not what she considers a perfect child, so it would be beyond her ability to give her what she needs; she is simply incapable of seeing beyond her own needs. It falls on me to protect my daughter. I'm her solid wall."

I nodded as if I understood, although I knew I couldn't, and he knew it as well. I had no idea of the challenges he faced as a single parent of a child with special needs. I didn't know what would become of our friendship, but whatever happened between us, Lena would be an essential part of it. He had trusted me enough to share this vulnerable, frightened part of himself, and I was grateful. "She's a beautiful, happy girl. That's clear to everyone who sees her, and you are doing an amazing job of raising her."

"But she'll be a full-time teenager soon and that is a particularly hard time for kids like Lena. Emotionally they're still children, but physically they're adolescents with all that means, and that scares me, too."

"If I'd been blessed with a child, I'd want to be the kind of parent you are," I said because it was the truth.

"You'd be a great mother; I can tell you that."

"Maybe someday," I said, not hiding the sorrow in my voice because that was the thing more than anything else Darryl and I had wanted.

Neither of us said much after that. I wondered if he was sorry he'd shared so much of himself and regretting it now. He was a private man; I could easily see that. His profession had taught him to keep his feelings hidden, not to show a vulnerability that might give an adversary an advantage. But I was not his adversary; I hoped he knew that. I suspected his wife had been. Yet there was nothing I could think of to say that would reassure him. We'd crossed a bridge that neither of us knew was there; there was no crossing back.

There was one truth about me, though, I wasn't ready to share. Darryl and I had been married a month before I told him about my gift—simply because there was no way to avoid it. Aunt Phoenix had made that clear on her third visit to our home, laden down with sage and other smelly things. She made it clear she wouldn't leave until he knew the truth, as mystifying as it was, about the women in our family.

"You need to tell him about the nutmeg and all the other stuff," she'd urged in a whisper. "Don't forget or I will."

I thought about that moment with a secretive smile remembering his astonished, accepting reaction. Darryl was as determined to understand every weird part of me as I was of him even though he had no strange quirks. Remembering that day, I wondered if its memory was why I now smelled nutmeg, which had become overpowering. I sneaked a look at Lennox focusing on the road ahead of us. He clearly didn't smell anything, but he did scowl and pull over to the side.

"Wonder what's going on here," he said to himself more than me. "Let me check it out and see what's going on."

"I think I'll come with you," I said. The nutmeg told me someone was dead, but who was it, the brother or sister? Had someone avenged Anna Lee's death?

Two police cars were parked behind a late-model BMW and black Range Rover near the space where Anna had been killed. On the ground nearby I spotted Harley's bouquet, the black-eyed Susans withered into yellowing stalks, leaving only a few pink roses identifiable. The remnants of Blade's flowers were still here, too, and I remembered the promise he'd made to Anna. I glanced down the dark road for any sign of his black truck, wondering if he had found a way to fulfill it.

Suddenly a wail of agony stunned us. Emily Delbarton, white linen trench coat dragging on the ground behind her, was walking in circles around the blue car, hands waving above her head.

"Why did you do it? My Eddie is dead! Why did you do it! Why? Why? For that little tramp?" Her questions screamed in anguish filled the night air, and the sound of her pain brought tears to my eyes. She ran into the road, wandering aimlessly as if hoping to follow her brother into death. An officer snatched her back, and she pulled away, running again to the BMW and trying to climb into the passenger seat. There was the screech of police cars and an ambulance pulled behind the parked cars, and another police officer, along with an emergency attendant, tried to ease Emily into the ambulance, but she was having none of it. She fought and screamed, her voice the only sound that could be heard.

"Let me see what I can find out," Lennox said, walking ahead of me. "I know some of these guys and they'll tell me what's going on."

"I'm going to get back in the car," I said. I'd had more than my share of uncomfortable encounters at crime scenes with the local police. Besides that, Edgar Delbarton's parting words had told me everything I needed to know:

> *At night-side I will lie down by her side.*
> *You will see. You will see. You will see me and*
> *my Annabel Lee. I will take what she has left me.*

Death was the gift his Annabel Lee had left him. He was lying down by her side at nighttime just as he said he would. Emily Delbarton's screams rang long and loud as she fought to stay close to the spot where her brother had taken his life. I covered my ears with my hands so I couldn't hear them.

"Well, so much for that," Lennox said when he got back in the car. His words shocked me at first, but a glance at his face told me that this was how he had learned to deal with calamity and heartbreak. He'd seen it so often he had learned to push it aside, made light of it, not let it touch him too deeply. "So here is what they think happened," he said, turning to me to explain. "Edgar Delbarton called his sister, Emily Delbarton, then decided to take his own life, making sure he did it before she was able to get there first. His way of paying her back, I guess. Nothing messy. Barbiturates and alcohol, they assume. Something he could time. They won't know for sure until they do an autopsy. He wanted his sister to find him. Must have hated her."

It was Emily who was the "Angel" dissevering his soul from his Annabel Lee. She was who he was paying back. I nodded as if I understood.

"They're pretty sure that it was Edgar Delbarton who killed Anna Lee, so if that's the answer you've been looking for, you've got it," Lennox said, as he pulled away from the crime scene. "It doesn't make much sense, but killings like these never do. Are you okay, Odessa?" he said, taking his eyes off the road to glance at me.

"Yeah, I guess so," I said. "But it still seems odd to me. He didn't strike me as a violent person, just crazy. Hitting somebody with your car, running them down, is a very brutal act. It would take planning, cunning, and a vicious streak that I didn't think he had."

"What about sending those roses? That seems vicious to me."

"That seems more passive-aggressive than violent."

"Well, like I've said before, you never know who is a killer until he has killed somebody, and that's what he did."

"It's an answer. Maybe one that will bring Harley some relief."

"It always does," Lennox said as his iPhone vibrated with a text. "That would be the lady who watches Lena wanting to know when I'm going to get home." His mind had quickly turned to his daughter as I knew it would, and we road in silence back to his place. He walked me to my car, and when we said good night we promised we'd meet for dinner at what had become our favorite Chinese restaurant. I wondered if he was sorry he'd been so forthcoming about his fears, and if it would make a difference between us. Time would tell, I decided, for both of us.

I called Harley when I got home. When he didn't answer, I left a message telling him I had news that I wanted to share in person. When I saw him, I'd explain as best I could what I knew about Anna and why she had been killed. This was bound to bring some peace, at least as much as possible.

As for Louella, I looked forward to seeing her tomorrow and left a message I'd be over in the morning. I was ashamed I'd actually suspected she might have had something to do with Anna's death. I hated to consider the possibility, but maybe Lennox's pessimistic take on wayward apples and trees had left more of an impression than I wanted to admit. I owed Louella an apology I knew I could never give. In lieu of that, I'd bake some muffins to surprise her and had enough chocolate chips left for that. I smiled to myself as I imagined Erika's delight. Whatever was bothering Louella was nothing compared to what I feared it might be. I slept peacefully that night, the first time in weeks, with Juniper nudging himself against my feet at the bottom of my bed like a cozy blanket.

Chapter 15

Whenever I visited Louella's home, I was momentarily pulled into the past; this house and I had history. Subtle odors flooded back—food left to burn, hopes abandoned, unhappiness as thick and lingering as a smell. This house belonged to Louella now, and those years and disturbing memories were finally beginning to fade. Despite her occasional setbacks, Louella, once a sad, troubled woman, was growing stronger and more self-confident. I breathed a sigh of relief when she opened the door. There was no hint of the dangerous glimmer she'd carried for so long, that reddish-purplish glow that once had made me cry, only the bleary-eyed, tired face of a weary young mother in need of a good night's sleep.

"Are those for me? Thanks for baking them. I really need this," she said when I handed her the platter of chocolate chip muffins. Her half smile, forced and quick, told me she was right.

"Straight from the oven to you, Erika, and Red." I gave her a hug, then followed her into her modest, spare kitchen where all the memories were good: coffee brewed with Red, giggles with Erika, *trying* to teach her how to cook.

"I've got good news to share. Great news!" I said as I sat down at the narrow kitchen table. "The cops know who hit Anna, who murdered her."

Louella slapped her hand over her mouth with a gasp. "Oh my God! Who was it? Why did he do it? When did they arrest him? Does Harley know?" The questions came in such rapid fire I couldn't answer them all. What's more, I wasn't ready to share more than I knew, which was only what I saw last night, and that was what I told her. "The killer was a guy named Edgar Delbarton, who she knew before she came to Risko's. A nutcase who was obsessed with her. They didn't arrest him because he killed himself on the road where Anna died. I left a message for Harley to call me."

"Did you say Delbarton? Isn't that the owner of—"

"Yeah, Delbarton Estates. Not the owner but the younger brother. He came to the open house, one of those people you couldn't forget." Louella had come into the office only twice since Anna's death and missed the roses drama. Vinton would eagerly fill her in on all the awful details when he saw her, and I didn't want to think about them, much less discuss all that had happened.

"Why? Why would he want to kill her? How do you hate somebody that much?"

"Who knows? Maybe he thought he loved her, or that was what he called it. Destructive emotions are sometimes mistaken for love because it's a feeling that means different things to each person and not always easy to know. When that happens, it can turn ugly and take a person to a bad place."

"Yeah, you're right about that," she said, her gaze quickly shifting from mine. "Feel like some coffee with the muffins?"

She boiled the water in a kettle and rinsed out the French press, a gift from me. Water never boils when you expect it. I waited impatiently as she carefully measured the coffee into the pot, added the water letting it steep longer than necessary, then finally plunging it. Whatever she was going to tell me, she was taking her own sweet time getting to it. But her glimmer was fine; they knew who killed Anna Lee and all was feeling right in the world. Nothing she could say would change any of that.

Louella put the muffins on the table along with milk, then poured the coffee into two stoneware mugs that Vinton had brought her back from his summer trip to Martha's Vineyard. Whenever Vinton went on one of his "little jaunts," as he called them, he made a point of bringing some token back for Louella, be it a vase, embroidered napkins, or decorative mugs. Vinton loved playing the role of indulgent parent, something Louella had sorely missed all her life. His newfound attention to Bella and Anna must have stung even though Louella would never admit it. It certainly hadn't driven her to murder. How could I have even considered it?

"You know how much we all love you, don't you?" I said, ashamed to think about that now.

Louella looked surprised. "What brought that on?"

"Well, nothing. Just wanted to remind you," I said, embarrassed to have mentioned it. "What is this life-changing news you wanted to discuss with me? I'm tired of waiting."

"Well, I made a big decision a couple of days ago."

I took a sip of coffee still hot enough to burn my tongue. "You want to tell me what it is or should I just go home?" I said, tired of hiding my impatience.

"Well, I know you might be mad about it, but I've gone back and forth until I knew for sure. It has to do with Red." She settled back into her chair and glanced at me to see my reaction. I saw a trace of tears in her eyes, reminding me again of her vulnerability and the many secrets she had shared.

"I'm fond of Red, but you are my friend," I said to reassure her.

"Ever since he's been back, claimed Erika as his child, come back into our lives, I was so sure about our future, and I'm not anymore."

"You two have been through a lot together," I said, recalling what I knew of their long history, parts of it troubled, to say nothing of the daughter they adored.

"I always thought of Red as my fiancé, even when I was afraid he was dead. But that's all changed now. I don't want to marry him. Last night, he asked me again for the tenth time when we were going to set a date, and I told him we weren't, that I'd changed my mind. I wanted to go my way, and he should go his."

I picked up a muffin, nibbled at the edge, trying to think of what to say, and finally came up with, "Are you absolutely sure?"

"I know how real love looks, and we don't have it," she said bluntly.

"What was Red's reaction when you told him?"

"Red is good at hiding his feelings. He didn't look me in the eye at first, so I couldn't tell what he was thinking, then stared at me hard and said if that's what I wanted, it was all right with him, but not to forget he would be picking *his* daughter up to take her to his mama's this morning. Calling her his daughter instead of Erika. Then he slammed the door and left."

I finished off my muffin before asking the obvious.

"What are you going to tell Erika?" More than once, the child had joyfully described the dress she planned to wear as flower girl at what she assumed would be their large, fancy wedding. She adored her father, who had quickly become a steadying influence after the considerable turmoil in her young life. Ericka was a strong child, but this was going to hit her hard.

Louella drew in a breath before telling me, "I don't know. I guess we have to let things settle down first, figure out when he's going to see her, how—" Without finishing her sentence, she looked off into the adjoining living room, then brought her gaze back to me. "I just want to be a good mother, better than my own was. I will never forget how angry she always was at me, and how deeply that hurt. I've been thinking a lot about my mom recently, what happened between us. Maybe it was Rosalie's visit that brought all this on. Whatever it was, Mom has been in my thoughts."

"Did you say Rosalie? Rosalie Davis? She came over here?" I didn't hide the surprise that verged on alarm. "What did she want?"

Puzzled by my reaction, Louella didn't answer right away. Instead, she took butter out of the refrigerator, spreading a thick layer on a muffin that didn't need any. Another delaying tactic. "She came over last Saturday, out of the blue. It was weird in a way, but it was nice, too. I know you don't like her—"

"I don't really know her, but she does seem to be a devoted daughter, to her father, that is." Rosalie's impromptu visit to Louella bothered me, but I wasn't sure why.

"Said she'd just come from seeing you, and you said to check with me about a memorial for Anna, that I might have some of Anna's stuff. I gave her Bella's and Harley's cell numbers and explained I didn't know Anna all that well. She told me nobody knew Anna all that well."

"That's a strange thing to say." I wondered what Rosalie was getting at.

She lowered her voice, ready to share a bit of gossip. "Did you know Anna used to work in a strip club before she came to Risko's?"

"Really?"

"Rosalie's company renovated property for a guy she knows who is a customer at the club and he told her." She paused as if she knew what I was thinking, then continued self-righteously, "I told her I didn't want to hear anything else because we all have things we're ashamed of, and that Anna was dead. But to tell the truth, Dessa, I was flattered that she told me; it was like we were really friends who share things, you know what I mean?"

"Rosalie had a lot of tales to tell to a newfound friend," I said, wondering what this visit was really about. "What else did she say?"

"Just asked if anyone was planning a memorial for Anna and said that she wanted to help plan it. That's really nice of Rosalie, isn't it? I can't wait to tell her that they know who killed Anna. I know she'll be glad to hear it because she asked if I'd heard anything."

Had Rosalie been in touch with Harley or Bella? What had she told them?

"I admire her, Dessa. She's like take-no-prisoners tough. I can learn a lot of stuff from somebody like her, how to make deals, how to dress classy. Rosalie wouldn't tie herself down to a man who wasn't bringing something tangible into her life." Avoiding my eyes again, she boiled more water, though we hadn't finished the coffee that was left in the pot.

"Red doesn't bring tangible stuff into your life?"

She hesitated as if considering it. "No. Not really."

"You need to choose your own friends, make your own decisions. Rosalie Davis may not be everything she seems, and *tangible* can mean many things." I sounded like the mother she didn't have; she ignored me like the hardheaded daughter she once had been.

"Rosalie wants us to start working together," she continued dreamily. "Isn't that something. She can be like a mentor. She asked about this house, too; it's old and everything, but she said she could reset it for me, and maybe I could sell it and reset my life!"

"Breaking up with your long-term lover and selling your mama's house are two decisions you don't want to make lightly," I warned, sounding more critical than I meant to. "All of this from one visit? She must have been here for quite some time. Did she mention why she visited me?"

"Not really. Said it was just to drop off a book and find out about Anna's memorial."

"She didn't mention my relationship with her father?"

"No. Maybe she was going to say something, but Erika came running downstairs then, gave me a kiss, and we got to talking about motherhood and mothers. I felt really close to Rosalie. Here I thought she was just some snotty rich girl, but we actually have a lot in common. Goes to show you can't go judging somebody on a first impression."

I sipped some coffee, took a healthy bite from my second muffin, wondering why Rosalie was dodging the truth. I'd gone out of my way *not* to mention Anna's friends, and she was aware of my relationship with Terrence. I was reasonably sure that she hadn't found out about Anna's past from some customer who frequented the club. These were small lies, but small lies always concealed bigger ones.

"What did Rosalie tell you about her mother?" I said just to be sure.

"Her mother is dead, died in childbirth. Her father raised her by himself. He loved her mother so much that he never got over her death, which is why he gave her the name her mother wanted for her. Lily was her mother's name, but she spelled it *Lil Lee*; that's such a pretty way to spell *Lily*. That was on Rosalie's birth certificate."

"She told you a lot about herself. What else did she say she found out?" Rosalie may have sensed her father wasn't telling her all she wanted to know about her mother. That was innocent enough but still puzzling.

"Just that her mother spelled her name *Rosa Lee;* that was on her birth certificate, not *Rosalie.* We had a good laugh about that and how people spelled my name *Lou Ella* until Mom set them straight. Mom did a lot of terrible things, but she was fierce when people got my name wrong."

A sliver of a thought, unformed, unreliable, came into my mind. When Erika ran into the kitchen nearly knocking over her father it disappeared as quickly as it came.

"Aunt Dessa! You're here! Are these for me?" She grabbed a muffin and bit off the top.

"For me, too, I hope," said Red, following behind her. He and Louella exchanged an uneasy look that made me turn back to Erika and consider the heartbreak that might come.

Red avoided my eyes, perhaps guessing what Louella had told me. "I've got some stuff to do upstairs; I'll be back down in a few," Louella said, leaving the kitchen after acknowledging him. He visibly relaxed after she was gone, sitting down where she had been, and I wondered if this was the way it would be between the three of us. They both had a place in my heart, alone or together.

"How you doing?" I asked Red after Louella was gone.

"I'll be okay." His glimmer had always been tender but also one of a man who could make his way in a street fight, if not in the world of words. Lucky for him, only I could see his vulnerability. The day I met him, it had gone from pale silver to soft pink, growing softer and paler whenever he was with his daughter. Thanks to the gift, I easily saw the truth of this large man who was fighting to be the best father he could be. His own had been a mean, brutal man, and Red did everything he could not to become like the man he hated.

"How about some coffee with that muffin," I said, as if the kitchen had become mine; his prompt smile showed he appreciated my presence.

"Sounds good to me."

"Me too," added Erika.

"Lots of milk, for her."

I poured the coffee, mostly milk for Erika, and watched the two solemnly drinking together. I'd told Red the day we met I'd heard it was good luck for a girl to look like her father and been touched by the relief that flooded his eyes. Erika certainly did look like him; there was no mistaking those grayish eyes and reddish skin dotted with freckles belonged to him as they did to his mother. It was how he recognized Erika the first time he saw her.

"Thank you, Dess," he said, his appreciation reaching further than pouring some coffee. I gave him a pat on the shoulder, less intrusive than the hug that had been my first impulse.

Louella rushed back into the room with library books and gave them to Erika. "Don't forget these," she said, ignoring Red.

"We'd better be on our way. I promised the general I'd take these books back before the library closes, and we're taking the bus."

"That's me, not Mom," said Erika in case there was any doubt. "Sometimes I'm the general; sometimes I'm the warden."

"Because she keeps me in line," Red said with a wink.

The bond between fathers and daughters was every bit as complex and deep as that between daughters and mothers. I loved my father dearly despite his aloofness. I knew he loved me although he never seemed completely at ease, as if unsure of what to say or make of his only child. I understand that dis-

tance now. Considering my mother, her sisters, and our peculiar gifts, I can hardly blame the man. I thought about Lennox
and Lena, and the revelation about his fear for his daughter
and his own future. I'd glimpsed a helplessness he fought hard
to keep hidden. And Terrence and Rosalie and the frightening display of her controlling love when she didn't get her
way. Anna came to mind then, and what Bella said of her futile search for a father.

"You're a good man, never doubt that!" I called out to
Red as he headed out the back door. Whatever happened between him and Louella, I wanted him to know my feelings.
Erika had no doubt. She delivered one of her warm, tight
hugs, and I held her closer than usual.

Later as Louella cleaned the kitchen, I asked the question
I'd wanted to ask since she'd told me her decision. "What happened between you and Red that changed things so quickly?"

"The point is what doesn't happen between us!" She sat
back down at the table and handed me her cell phone. "Here,
take a look at these and you'll see what I mean. Bella sent
these a few days ago. They're of Harley and Anna. Just look at
them! When I saw them I realized what true love really looks
like and what is gone between me and Red. Passion! Excitement for each other. Look at how happy they are. You can't
hide that. We don't have that kind of love and never will!"

"Well, all couples look happy like that when their pictures
are taken," I said halfheartedly, but saw what she was talking
about.

Bella had taken dozens of photographs, some obviously
candid, and there was no mistaking that love was what you
saw. My throat tightened at the reminder of Harley's loss.
Some were selfies, the two of them giggling at dinner, playfully scowling, mugging it up; simply viewing Anna's laugh-

ing face again stirred my heart. One taken of Anna preparing to jog stopped me short; how long after that had she been killed? This was a haunting vision, Anna smiling at Bella as she bent down to check her sneakers. It was followed by a video of Anna in a bright red sweat suit, gulping a bottle of Evian, grinning, offering it to Bella as if saying, "This one's for you," and maybe the thought of those words were what made it all come together, quickly and with such intensity.

I paused the video, capturing her face, lingering on it, wondering how I could have missed it except for willful forgetting of the past that prevented me from seeing the obvious. Her round, plump face might bring to mind a cute chipmunk for some who wanted to see her beauty, but for others, like my aunt, the observance of a "weak chin" would remind them of the boyish face that belonged to her father. Other things should have told me. Their avoidance of sweets. Diabetes could be genetic. The troubled mother Anna deemed "nuts," the same Lil, as Terrence called her—Lil Lee as Rosalie discovered—who said she was taking one of her twin daughters for herself and leaving the other for you, giving each child a bit of herself in their names: Annabel Lee and Rosa Lee.

"Do you see what I mean?" Louella said, taking back her phone. I was too lost in thought to speak. "That's how those photos affected me, too!"

"Well, you don't want to make any rash decisions." I offered only half a thought because my mind had left Louella and taken flight.

"Well, I'm eager for a change."

"For Erika's sake, give it some time! Wait a few weeks and see how you feel. You have a kid; don't break her heart because you admire a woman you don't know and have seen a couple of pictures!"

"Wow, you're not holding back, are you?" Louella said, obviously hurt.

"I know it because it's the truth," I said, speaking to Louella but talking about Terrence and his daughters. And it *was* the truth, I was certain of that. I didn't say more to Louella about what was really on my mind, but my unspoken thoughts stayed with me all the way home.

Chapter 16

The moment I walked in the door, Aunt Phoenix, sensing my trouble in mind, sent one of her irritating, ominous texts:

A tomato may be a fruit, but don't put it in a fruit salad.

I sat down, counted to ten, and called her.

"This one beats the rose and monkey. What are you trying to tell me? In plain English, please," I said, annoyed but amused.

She chuckled her deep-throated laugh that either puts me at ease or raises my hackles. "You've got the power, you've got the gift, you figure it out," she said.

It was the hackles this time. "Thanks for nothing, Aunt Phoenix."

"You're welcome," she said politely, and hung up.

"As if I don't have enough on my mind," I said louder than necessary into the dead phone, which promptly got the attention of Juniper, who thought I was talking to him. Tail waving high in the air, he rushed toward me hoping for an afternoon snack. It was past time for my lunch, too, but I

wasn't hungry. I was coffee-ed out for the day, so I made myself a cup of green tea instead, remembering what Celestine
had said about it being good for clear thinking and focusing
your mind; then I settled down at the kitchen table to figure
things out.

My aunt was right, though I hated to admit it. Knowing
that a tomato is a fruit didn't mean you should mix it up with
apples, oranges, and cantaloupe. Simply possessing knowledge didn't mean you had to share it. It was similar to one of
Darryl's favorite sayings, that knowledge was knowing what
to say, wisdom was knowing when to say it. My problem, I
wasn't sure how wise I was.

What did I owe Terrence Davis? Was it my place to share
my suspicions about a woman now deceased who may have
been his daughter? I suspected that Rosalie may also have de-
duced the truth. Anyone who knew Terrence well would
have immediately spotted Anna's resemblance. And there was
Lil Lee, Anna and Rosalie's mother, and a genetic disposition
toward diabetes, which may be why Terrence avoided sweets
and watched his diet. There may have been something on
Rosalie's birth certificate as well that made her consider that
truth.

Bella had said she and Anna had become good friends with
Rosalie when they met at Delbarton, and Anna may have
been as candid with Rosalie as she had been with Bella. The
two of them had hovered protectively over Anna as devotedly
as sisters when she returned to the open house after fleeing in
fear, forgetting even to tell Harley why she had left. I knew
now it was the sight of Edgar Delbarton, pursuing her to her
death.

Rosalie had been hungry for anything I could say about
her mother, for any connection to her past. Maybe Anna had
shared what she knew, filling in the clues for which Rosalie
had been searching. Her relentless commitment to Anna's

memorial and desire to reach out to Anna's friends may have been her way of reaching out to a sister she only now realized she no longer had.

Had Rosalie shared her suspicions with her father? She was protective of his well-being and wouldn't want to burden a dying man with a painful remembrance from his past. Terrence's words to me made it clear that even if somebody reached out to him now, it was too late. He needed comfort, and his daughter would see to that.

No doubt he had shared those thoughts with Rosalie more than once and she had decided to grant him any peace he needed. Neither she nor I knew the complete truth about Anna's connection to Terrence. Too many pieces were missing, Anna was dead, and it was too late to fit anything together. Too late for Terrence as well. This was a family secret about a woman he despised and who had abandoned her child. It was time to let the past go, and I had to do the same.

A tomato may be a fruit, but don't put it in a fruit salad.

All I could share was what I knew for sure, and that was what had happened last night. I called Harley to tell him I knew. The hoarseness in his voice told me he had been crying and had already found out.

"I talked to Louella late this morning. She told me you had just left. I just . . . I don't know what to say, what to feel."

"I'm sorry I didn't tell you myself, but—"

"No, it's okay. Louella said that talking about it takes her mind off something she's worried about; she's been calling everyone to let them know. Bella, Vinton, Tanya, Rosalie Davis, that woman from Delbarton. Anna's gone, so it doesn't matter all that much."

Silence is a healing thing and that was what was needed, both of us holding our phones for a while, saying nothing, me waiting for Harley to speak first.

"I need to know more about this guy who killed her. Why he did it. How you found out. I have questions about everything and I need to understand, about Anna, about this . . . I just need to talk to somebody before I go crazy."

"Yeah, sure, I'm not going anywhere. I'll be here whenever you come to talk, and I'll tell you what I know."

"There was something else, too, I need to talk to you about, something that might be important. I finished going through Anna's things and there were some letters she wrote that came back to her unopened, and I'm not sure what to do with them, if I should try sending them again. Can I come by later and show them to you?"

"Sure, I'll be here," I said, waiting for him to hang up before I did.

It was good that Louella was sharing what she knew about Anna's killer, good news needed to be shared, and those who loved Anna would want to know that a question about her death was finally resolved. Maybe that would offer a bit of peace to everyone, and it was time to begin planning a memorial. I'd bring it up as gently as I could to Harley when he got here tonight, and bring Rosalie into it as well, give her the chance to find her own peace with Anna, whatever that peace was.

It was going on four before I realized just how hungry I was, and hunger came on with a vengeance as it tends to do. It was too late for lunch, too early for dinner, so I made my favorite meal-in-a-minute sandwich: tuna fish on a toasted English muffin. When the first call came, I didn't recognize the number so I didn't bother answering. I answered the second time and heard heavy, labored breathing on the other end of the line. An obscene call as the day was ending? Just what I needed, and last thing in this world I felt like hearing. I answered with a few choice curse words that I rarely use, and hung up again. Five minutes later, he called again.

"Odessa, please, please, don't hang up, please." His voice was so weak I could barely hear it, and it took me a minute to recognize it.

"Terrence?"

"Yes, it's me. There is nobody here. I don't know anybody else to call. Please don't hang up again."

"Let me call Rosalie."

"No! Don't call her, please don't call her, not yet."

"Are you in danger? Let me call the police or—"

"No!" he said loudly, using whatever voice he had left. He stopped talking, breathing hard, catching his breath. "No, no cops! Not them. I just need to figure something out, that's all. I just need to talk things out. With somebody. I don't have or know anybody else. Are you there, Odessa? Are you still there?"

"Yes, I am," I said, wondering to myself why in the world I was.

"Do you remember how we met, Odessa? How close we were, how much we loved each other? Don't you remember?"

I didn't answer. If he was trying to blackmail me into acknowledging some debt from our past, he had misjudged me and this moment. Yet I'd chosen to allow him and what we had shared back into my life. I had ignored Phoenix's advice about letting sleeping dogs and unturned stones just lie. Once you've seen it, you can't pretend you didn't, you can't forget what you found out was there, she'd said. I couldn't pretend now not to hear the broken voice of a man I once loved. That part of myself that my *Star Trek*–loving husband, Darryl, loved, what he called "the empath Deanna Troi," was still inside me, and she along with my mother's spirit, what must have been the kinder edge of the gift, warned that you never ignore the last plea of a dying man, particularly one you once loved.

"What do you need?" I asked, the empath Odessa having her say.

"Just for you to listen to me, listen until I stop talking and have said what is on my mind."

"Okay, I won't leave. I won't hang up."

"Do you promise, on everything we have been?"

It came down to two things: kindness and memory. I had no choice but to keep my word. We had both been so young and he was right; we had meant so much to each other. I closed my eyes, trying to remember it all: the black-eyed Susans from his grandmother's garden, brought to me when I least expected them in a bunch tied with a red ribbon. His shy smile as he thrust them into my hands. For the first time in years, I'd thought of them when I saw the bouquet Harley had brought for Anna. So many other things: our discoveries of old movies we'd never seen; of slow dancing to vinyl records from his grandmother's collection—Nat King Cole, Billie Holiday, Dinah Washington—played on her old record player. Silly jokes we remembered from childhood, laughing and teasing each other like kids do, boisterously with no embarrassment. They were memories, unique ones, that could only have belonged to us in that time and place. I had let it all in, the good as well as the bad, and neither could be forgotten. His wounds were as deep as mine, maybe deeper. I had gone on from there, wiser because I had known him, found a good man I loved, been happy. He had held on to that past and the anguish that it brought.

His breathing was labored and slow, each breath taking more from him. "Terrence, are you okay?" I dreaded what I might hear.

"No! No! No!" His voice was more strained and fearful each time he said it, as if he was talking to somebody else and he'd forgotten I was there. His line went dead. I called Rosalie, despite his plea. He may not have wanted to worry her, but this was a time for her to worry. It was puzzling, though, why he called me and not his daughter. Had pride come into it? Did they have another fight? There was no answer, so I left a message that her father sounded ill and that she should get to his home as soon as possible. I considered calling the police, then thought better of it. He'd been so adamant about not doing it he must have had a good reason. I tried calling him again, then gave up. I realized then that I had no choice. I'd have to go to his home, check on him in person, make sure he was okay. What did I owe Terrence Davis? I asked myself for the second time today. I wasn't sure, but whatever it was, my final debt was about to be paid.

Hopefully, Rosalie had gotten my message and would be there waiting for me and she would take care of whatever was necessary. I would be free then to thank him for the book he'd given me and be on my way as quickly as possible, free of unpaid dues and unturned stones.

It was still afternoon, but the house looked closed down, all the lights off, all the shades pulled down. I remembered then that the bedrooms were filled with artwork and other collectibles that had to be kept free of sunlight and extremes in temperature. Nevertheless, there was a deathly still about the place as if it had been deserted, which was alarming, since I'd spoken to Terrence less than an hour before. Rosalie may have gotten my message and come to her father's aid, taken him to an emergency care clinic or hospital and he was now safe. I hoped that was so.

I rang the doorbell twice, then stepped back to get a better view of the house and possibly see somebody in one of the bedrooms. A light suddenly turned on, then off, almost as if giving a signal, letting me know that somebody was there. I rang the bell again to see if the light went on again, but there was nothing.

"Terrence, are you there?" I called from the street up to

the house. I tried the door this time, hoping maybe it had been unlocked, which of course it hadn't. Not everybody was as careless as my aunt. "Terrence!" I called again, then stepped back. The light came on and stayed this time, telling me that he might be in trouble and unable to get to the door. I knew from my past experiences of selling split-levels that this was not the only way into the house; the garage was another way in. Jana Mae had mentioned Rosalie cursing out a locksmith about a broken lock. Maybe he'd taken his own sweet time coming back to repair it, and if that was the case, it was my way in. Lennox's disapproving face popped into my mind at the prospect of breaking and entering. At best, an uninvited entrance into this house might be called trespassing; at worst, a felony. But I had been invited by the owner, in a matter of speaking, and if Terrence was in danger it was my responsibility to check on him. At least, I had to give this a try. Where was my mother's amulet when I needed it? Hanging on a hook near the mirror in my bedroom, high enough for Juniper not to reach it and me to pass by without seeing it. It was too late now to worry about a protective charm; I'd have to take my chances. I glanced up and down the street making sure nobody was watching, then cautiously made my way to the back of the house.

A garage is a garage, but this was an exceptionally large one, built long and wide enough for at least three cars. Two double garage doors both with dark wood paneling enclosed it, and were obviously heavy enough to only be opened with a remote opener. I spotted a flag-stone path leading to the back of the structure and after another quick glance behind me followed the path. It led down a walkway, overgrown by bushes and weeds, to a side door leading to the garage yet possible to see from the street. This hidden entrance must be the one Rosalie wanted to make sure was secured. I knocked on the door first, habit more than anything else, and then entered the garage, which lit up with motion sensitive lights when I walked in.

"Terrence?" I called again, for good measure even though I doubted he'd hear me. It was a large well-lit space and I anxiously looked for the stairway that led to the inside of the house. At best, that door might be unlocked; at worst, I could yell and bang and maybe get his attention. Surprisingly, there was only one car parked in the oversized space, leaving ample space for me to make my way to the stairs. It was one of those vintage cars that Terrence had said he collected, long and black with an elegant grill that belonged in another era. A gangster's car made for show, if ever there was one. Lennox's words about the car he'd seen and his long-gone days arresting the bad guys came to mind and made me smile. Like most people, Lennox Royal had aspects of himself it would take a lifetime to know. I edged past the car, then stopped, turned around to look. Something red had caught my eye. It was a bit of torn fabric, barely noticeable at first, that looked as if it had been snatched from a piece of clothing and welded by force into the middle of this fancy grill.

"Anna!" I uttered her name out loud without realizing I had said it. I touched the grill of the car, then the fabric, caressing it with my fingers, praying it would give up any piece of information it was still holding.

It was the gift that told me what I had to know, as it had done at the place where she had died, whispering into my soul in a way I could barely hear, and it was as clear as it had been on the road that day when I knelt in the dirt and could feel what was left of her spirit. I knew for certain what had happened to her and how it had happened. I could feel the hard, brutal steel of the car, the utter surprise she must have known, the horror that had taken her young life before she felt the peace that would finally claim her.

"Anna!" I said her name, whispered it this time because I knew what had happened. How she had died. Who had killed her. I heard Rosalie on the stairs. She came down slowly, carefully, from inside the house, each step purposefully taken. I backed away from the car, touching the space that had touched Anna, saying a last good-bye. And I remembered Lennox's warning words, of not knowing who a killer was until he had killed.

Chapter 17

"What do you want? Why are you here? Get out now!" Rosalie spoke with the same quiet rage I'd heard when she argued with her dying father in her studio that day.

"Terrence called and I came to check on him. Well, you're here now, so I know that everything must be okay. Give him my greetings and I'll be on my way," I said, my voice cheerful, nonthreatening, hiding my fear. I stepped farther back from the car, shifted my gaze to the ceiling above her head, anything but her face, pulling my lips into a grimace of a smile. She crossed the space between us, stared at the car grill, then at me. I forced myself to look into her eyes, which were holes of darkness.

"Did you get my message?" I tried to take the tremor out of my voice.

"What are you talking about?" Her voice had no tone.

"The one about your father. Terrence. I called because I was worried about him and came over to check on him, and that's why I am here."

"There was no message."

"Is he okay? He wasn't doing well when he called me," I said, ignoring her response.

"He called you?" Her eyes widened with surprise. I didn't know whether that was good or bad because I couldn't tell what was going on in her mind. "My father is fine. I just checked him. He's asleep now, and he'll stay that way until I wake him."

"Okay, that's good news." I tried not to see those eyes and wondered how I could make my way out of there.

"Here is what I know," she said, abruptly turning away from me as if speaking to somebody who had just walked into the cavernous garage. "I could hear a noise and thought somebody had broken into our house and come in through the garage. As a woman on her own with a sick father upstairs, I was frightened. I decided to come downstairs and check, and I got the gun from his antique collection. I loaded it because I was afraid. I came down here and that is when I found you, somebody I didn't immediately recognize." She pointed the gun toward me, making sure I could see it. "It's a collector's item, but it shoots."

I know little about guns except that I'm scared of them, and I was frightened at the sight of this small weapon with its pearl handle and designs on its barrel. It was small but deadly. Guns, no matter how old, always were.

"You have been caught trespassing," she continued in a matter-of-fact voice. "When I call the police, I will tell them that I shot an intruder. I'll explain that the lock on the door leading in here had been broken for several days, and could be accessed from the street. They will say that I had the right to defend myself, and that will be the end of it."

"What will the police say when they see the front of that car, how it's been smashed, when they see that piece of red fabric still attached to it?" I had no doubt now that she understood what I'd seen and that I knew what had happened. No more pretense was necessary. Was Terrence still alive? Had she killed him, too? It would be an easy thing for her to do. A pillow over the head of a dying man too sick to put up a struggle. A sip of something that would shorten his life. But I smelled no nutmeg, no hint of it. I was grateful for that. That meant he might come downstairs, make his way into the garage, and this would be over.

"I hit a deer, a very big one, a couple of weeks ago and it bled profusely. I tried to wipe the blood off before my father saw it, and a piece of the red cloth I used must have gotten stuck. It's a vintage car and I parked it in here so my father could have it properly repaired. It's difficult to find technicians who have those skills. A grill like that is not easily replaced." There was no emotion or sorrow, which was scarier even than the gun. Her glimmer was puzzling the first time I saw it, but now I could distinguish the colors, dark and foreboding with what I'd heard my aunt call an evilness to the boundaries, a description I'd only heard once. Rosalie had killed Anna, and she would kill me. I had no doubt about that.

"Rosalie, I think you should put the gun down before you do something else you will regret." My plea was halfhearted because I sensed my words would make no difference. "There are tests the police run that will determine what you killed wasn't a deer but a person. They will see that car and . . ."

"And what?" she said, aiming the gun at me again. "When the police come, it will be because I called them. They will come into this garage, glance at the grill of this beautiful old car, and say it's a shame a deer could do so much damage. I talked to your friend Louella this morning and she said they know who killed Anna because he killed himself. The question of Anna Lee's death is over. Their only question will be why you were in my garage, and you won't be here to explain."

I wondered why I'd never before noticed that deadness in her eyes, not at the open house, in her studio nor even in my living room. I'd missed that the same as I had the hints that Anna Lee was Terrence's other daughter.

"Does your father know about the car? He may not know who you killed, but he suspects you hit somebody, which is why he didn't want me to call the police. He's protecting you, isn't he?"

"My father loves me, and I love him. We protect each other. Always. From everyone who tries to separate us, who will do us harm."

"Will he still protect you when he knows you killed his other daughter, your sister?"

"I don't know what you're talking about," she said, but I caught a glimpse of something I hadn't seen before, a twitch of her eye that I had missed. I studied her closely, figuring out the best way to go forward, come up with the thing that would convince her not to kill me, maybe even to let me go.

"How did it make you feel when you found out that Anna Lee was your fraternal twin?" I said it gently, as if talking to a wayward child in need of convincing and comfort, trying to reach a piece of her I wasn't certain was there. It was the way Darryl would speak to a child who was desperate and had nothing to live for. A kid whom other people had given up on, assuming he or she was beyond hope and help. I called upon that part of me, that tender part of myself my husband had loved.

She took a breath and then another short one, and I prayed that I was getting through.

"I don't have a sister," she said as if she believed it.

"You're right, Rosalie. Nobody knows that for sure. Not me, not you." I tried to keep my voice from shaking. "But if you had, Anna would have been the perfect one. You had to have felt some connection with her, even a small one. Something you may have grown to love. I wish you had gotten a chance to do that."

"Well, I didn't," she said, with a defensiveness I hadn't

heard before. She was holding the gun, but it was aimed at the floor, not me. I realized then that she hadn't yet made up her mind about killing me, that a shot would wake up her father and she didn't want him down here. Maybe she hadn't figured out what to say when he found me dead. If Terrence was alive, so was I for the time being, but I had to keep her talking, convince her there was another way out.

"What do you mean?" she said, curious now, her face softening. "What do you mean about Anna and me, about getting to know her?"

"Do you remember at the open house, when Anna was frightened by that guy and you and Bella brought her aside to comfort her? It was like you and Bella were sisters, hovering over her, making sure she was okay. When the three of you went for that ride, I know you must have felt something then, talking and joking with her. Fraternal twins have a connection. It's not as strong as between that of identical twins, but you can't ignore it."

She looked lost for a moment, dropped her head, as if something new had occurred to her.

"Remember at my house when you asked about your mother? Anna was part of her, too. She must have loved you both, that was why she gave you both her name, her twin daughters who were nothing alike, but she wanted you to have that in common."

She shook her head as if shaking out a memory, and I realized then that I'd hit something else.

"There's still time for redemption, Rosalie. Maybe you didn't mean to kill her; maybe—"

"No," she said. "You don't know me very well."

"No, I don't. But I know your father, and how much he loves you. I know how much he loved your mother." That was a boldfaced lie and I hoped he hadn't told her the truth like he'd told it to me. "There are ways the two of you can fight this. He will do anything to protect you; you know that as well as I do."

She smiled slightly and nodded in agreement. "You're right. I do know that. My father loves me and has always loved me and always will."

"I don't know much about the law, but I do know that there are two justice systems and justice can be bought when there's money on the table. Your father will spend his fortune making sure that you are free, that anything you need will be taken care of. Don't make things worse by killing me along with your sister. There will be no way out of this then."

Terrence came downstairs cautiously, the wary steps of a man afraid he might fall or hear something he didn't want to know. It wasn't until he spoke, his voice low and frightened, that we both turned to face him.

"Rosalie, what is going on? Odessa, why are you here?"

"I'm here because you called me, Terrence. I wanted to make sure you were okay."

"Thank you. But Rosalie is here now. What else is going on—"

"You never told your father about Anna, did you?" I interrupted him, stronger now because of his presence. "She never told you, did she? You don't know."

"Don't know what? Rosalie, tell me what Odessa is talking about. Why do you have that gun? Put it back where it was before somebody gets hurt."

"Daddy, don't believe anything she says, whatever she tries to tell you."

"Terrence, don't believe me; believe your grandmother about Lil. Miss Evelyn suspected it and maybe you did, too, deep inside, that there were two baby girls, not just the one she left. Remember what she wrote: 'This one's for you!' She took your other daughter because that was how she meant to hurt you."

The mention of his grandmother knocked him off-balance, but he caught himself on the railing, managing to sit down on the last step before he fell. It took him a frighteningly long time to catch his breath enough to speak.

"Lil was disturbed in a lot of ways. I told you that. She left that to get even with me, that's all. She was out of her mind anyway. Like my mother was."

"But maybe she wasn't. That other child may have been searching for you the same way you were searching for her, on the same genetic sites, using her DNA to find her birth father, and maybe she found you, wrote you, but you never got those letters. Ask Rosalie about them. She goes through all your mail, pays the bills, knows what comes and goes. Tell him, Rosalie. It's time for him to know the truth." I spoke patiently, an understanding adult getting information from a recalcitrant child.

"I don't know what she is talking about," said Rosalie, but it was clear to both of us that she did.

"Her name was Anna. Anna Lee. Like Rosa Lee. And Lil Lee," I said.

"Rosalie? Did someone named Anna Lee write me?"

Rosalie wouldn't look her father in the eye, and Terrence had raised his daughter long enough to know what that meant. He knew from years of watching and loving her when she was hiding something from him, when she was lying.

"Rosalie, do you know where she is? Do you still have those letters? We need to reach out to her now, to make up for all this time. Have you been in touch with her? Can we—"

"She's dead, Daddy," Rosalie said, stopping him before he could finish. "She died a few weeks ago."

"Dead?" he said as if he couldn't believe it, didn't want to. His expression changed from curiosity to regret, then finally grief. He had found someone precious only to lose her. The worst was yet to come, and if Rosalie didn't tell him, I knew I would have to. I owed Anna that, owed him that, too.

"Tell him," I said.

Rosalie began to cry, covering her face with her hands like the little girl who knew how to charm her father into letting her do what she wanted, shaking her head, like a child does to keep from admitting some mischievous act, but there was no mischief here and no getting out of it. I was here to see to that.

"How did she die?" Terrence asked with such foreboding I suspected that he already knew.

"Somebody hit her when she was jogging. Hit her hard enough to kill her," I said.

"They found out who did it, Daddy. They know who killed her," said Rosalie quickly, unconvincingly. "It was this guy she worked for. I got to know her before she died, and—"

"What happened, Rosalie? You need to tell me what happened to this girl!" He knew her well enough to know she was lying.

"Her named was Anna, Terrence, and if you saw her picture you would know her immediately. With your chin, with diabetes like your grandmother may have had, with a rambunctious laugh like yours, the one that died years ago."

He looked from me back to Rosalie. "You need to tell me what happened," he repeated, then glanced at the car and began to sob, covering his mouth with his hands trying to hold it inside.

"I'm sorry, I'm sorry," Rosalie said, begging like she'd probably done all her life to get what she wanted. "Please forgive me, Daddy; please forgive me."

"Why didn't you tell me?"

"Because I didn't want you to know."

"Why did you kill her? Was it the money? You know how much we have. There's more than enough to share with anybody who needs it. Was it the artwork? When I'm gone, you could have done whatever you wanted with it." He was still on the stairs, unable to go any farther, and he could clearly see the grill of his car, and his daughter's face.

They had forgotten I was there, but I watched her, too, checking for the gun, still pointing toward the floor and not at me. I tried not to see the fragment of cloth still on the grill, but my eyes were pulled toward it and to what she had done. Had it been his money? I wondered, recalling that violent argument they had had about his art collection and what would become of it.

"No. It's never been any of that, Daddy. Never," Rosalie answered my unasked question.

"Then why?" Terrence pulled himself up to face his daughter, taking a step toward her, then others, each one taking more of a toll than the one before it, until he stood close enough to embrace her. "Why? Rosalie. If you knew she was your sister, why did you kill her?"

"There was no room for her in our lives, Daddy. It's always been the two of us, me and you. There was no space. I didn't have a choice because I love you so much." Her words hung over each of us. Rosalie looking relieved as if she had come to terms with her truth. Terrence grabbing his daughter, holding her tightly as she buried her head in his chest. Me watching the two of them, wondering what would happen next, knowing she still held that gun, which didn't bode well for me.

"Rosalie, you need to give the gun to your father now. You don't need it anymore. Your father knows what happened. Give him the gun and this will be over." It was a chance, but I had no choice but to take it.

Rosalie drew out of her father's embrace, stepped back, quickly glanced at me, then away. Fear crawled back into the hollow of my back.

"It will never be over," she said, turning away from me to face her father. "Daddy, listen to me. Nobody needs to know what happened. Nobody knows this but us. Nobody else is here."

"What are you saying?" Terrence glanced at me, then away, backing away from his daughter, stumbling back toward the stairs. "You don't mean that."

"We look out for each other, Daddy, how many times have you told me, have you said that to me? We are a team, and that's what we will always be. Please, Daddy. How many times have you told me that there is nothing I could do that you couldn't, wouldn't, forgive? Was that all a lie?"

"Rosalie—"

They were talking between themselves as they had always done, figuring things out. Father and daughter together. I was no longer there, and I knew that.

"I will call the police because there was an intruder. I shot the person and you came down, and that will be the end of it. Then it will be over."

I stared at Terrence, stunned and not wanting to believe what I'd just heard. He moaned, falling into himself as if he'd been kicked.

"Terrence?" He didn't seem to hear me.

But Rosalie had, and she continued what she had started. "This woman is part of your past like Anna was, Daddy. I'm your present and your future. You have to let her go the same way I did Anna. You have to do that."

"Don't do this, Terrence. Have you forgotten what we had, how much we loved each other?" I said. Hating to hear myself beg, I used the same words he'd said to me earlier: "Do you remember how we met? How close we were, how much we loved each other? Don't you remember?"

When he finally turned to face me, his eyes were filled with a deep sorrow that pricked my heart and made mine water. There was regret, there was no doubt of that, but overpowered by the love he felt for his daughter; that was unmistakable. For every distant memory he'd shared with me, there were a thousand recent ones he'd shared with his child. He had given his daughter everything she ever asked for, dedicated his life to her well-being, and he knew she was right. She was his present and future. He had no choice but to do what she told him because he had raised her to be who she was and there was nothing he could do now to change or stop her.

She kissed his forehead like the dutiful daughter she was.

"Daddy, please go back upstairs, and go back to bed. Try to go to sleep, and I will take care of this and call you when it is over, after I have called the police. This is the only way this can end, the best ending for both of us."

He turned slightly, as if deciding to make his way back, then stopped abruptly and turned to gaze at me.

It was at that moment, just before I met his eyes, that we all heard it: the unmistakable sound of a Harley motorcycle pulling up to the garage, and then the pounding of its namesake on the door yelling my name at the top of his lungs.

"Dessa! Dessa Jones! I know you're in there because your iPhone is. Dessa, answer me now. Are you okay?"

Rosalie glanced at me and then at her father. None of us spoke or moved. Everything turned still and silent.

"I know somebody is in there. Dessa?"

I closed my eyes unwilling to look at either of them, praying that Harley wouldn't leave, would stay where he was.

"Dessa, if you don't answer me, I'm going to assume that you're in trouble, and I'll call the police. Do you understand? Say something now!"

I held my breath unable to breathe, waiting for Harley to make his move and he did.

"I just called the cops. I told them it was an emergency. They're on their way," he said, his voice was louder than it needed to be.

"Give your father the gun," I said to Rosalie as calmly as I could. "This is over. My friend has called the police. That's the only choice you have now."

Terrence gently took the gun away from his daughter and tucked it into his robe. Rosalie nestled beside him, protected until the end.

"Forgive me, Odessa," Terrence whispered. I didn't look at him because I didn't want to see what had come into or left his eyes. I listened as he called his attorney, and as soon as the garage door was opened I ran away from them both.

Fortunately, the detectives were unaware of Risko Realty's dicey reputation and trouble-prone employees. I told them I was a family friend who had been locked in the garage, without mentioning how or why. Harley, never one to spend more time with cops then necessary, said he'd thought I was in trouble, but everything seemed to be okay. It was clear that the detectives were far more interested in the wealthy businessman, his pretty daughter, and the famous attorney who was on his way than they were in us.

When I got outside, I drew in the warm night air, gazed at the stars beginning to fill the sky, said a prayer of gratitude for my life. I'd been in there for less than an hour, but it seemed forever.

"What were you doing hanging out in that garage with

the reset girl and her daddy? Are you really okay?" Harley said skeptically as soon as he got the chance.

"Thank you for making me download that app on my phone and coming to find me," I said without answering.

"I was on my way over here anyway. One of Anna's returned letters had this address on it, and when the app showed you were here, too, I had to check it out. Do you know why she was writing this guy?" He studied my face searching for an answer but all I gave him was a shaky smile.

"Can you give me a ride home? I'm not up to driving," I said.

"If you're asking for a ride on my bike, then something serious must have gone down in there, and I want to hear about it," he said, handing me a helmet.

"Give me a day or two, and I promise to tell you everything." There was no way I could say that the car that killed his love and the woman who killed her were both inside that garage. Or that Terrence Davis was my first love as well as being Anna Lee's long-lost father and none of us had guessed the truth. It would all need to wait until I had the energy to tell it, and he had the strength to take it in. Harley pulled away from the curb, I closed my eyes, and we sped down the road. After the hell I'd been through, a fast ride on his noisy bike was as close to heaven as I could get.

"You are a forgiving woman, Dessa Jones," Lennox said as we finished dinner at our usual spot. "Terrence Davis's daughter held you as a prisoner, threatened you with a gun, scared you half to death. Why didn't you tell the authorities everything that happened? Why did you forgive her?"

I took a sip of tea because I wasn't sure myself. Maybe it had to do with that text my aunt had sent me from her favorite writer, shortly after it all happened:

It's one of the greatest gifts you can give yourself, to forgive. Forgive everybody. You are relieved of carrying that burden of resentment.

It had been more than a month since Anna Lee's murder. Rosalie had pleaded guilty, was going to prison, and would be there a while. Despite her father's money. My aunt had forgiven me for not wearing my amulet. (Probably the source of her text.) Louella had forgiven Red for simply being who he was, and I had forgiven Terrence, though it had taken a minute.

"Forgive me, Odessa," he had whispered that day, and it still haunted me. Forgive him for what? For choosing his daughter's well-being over my life? For what he had done or was about to do? What if Harley hadn't come? Was Terrence asking my forgiveness for the past or present? If I had truly forgiven him years ago, not held on to my anger, would I have known Anna was his daughter the moment I saw her? I had to forgive myself, too.

"Grace becomes you," Lennox said when I didn't answer his question.

"Grace becomes everyone," I said, and poured myself more tea. "Now will you forgive *me* for taking this last dumpling?" I asked, and we broke out laughing.

Dessa's Delightful Chocolate Chip Muffins

Life is easier when you share a chocolate chip muffin (or half a dozen) with a special somebody in unexpected circumstances—be it a kitchen or club of ill repute. This is a recipe that can be baked in a hurry, and the muffins are small enough to gobble a couple down with absolutely no shame.

Here's what you need:

Nonstick cooking spray
1¾ cups all-purpose flour
⅔ cup sugar
2 teaspoons baking powder
¼ teaspoon salt
¾ cup milk
¼ cup melted butter
1 lightly beaten egg
1 cup semisweet chocolate chips

1. Begin by buttering or spraying with nonstick cooking spray a 12-cup muffin tin.
2. Preheat the oven to 350 degrees F.
3. Measure your dry ingredients—flour, sugar, baking powder, salt—and whisk together in a mixing bowl.
4. In a smaller bowl, measure the liquid ingredients—milk, butter, egg—and whisk them together, too.
5. Now easy-peasy (whatever that means), pour the wet ingredients into the dry ones and mix until *gently* combined—not too much or you'll overmix it. Then fold in the chocolate chips.
6. Spoon the batter into the muffin tins and bake for 20 minutes, or until a toothpick poked in the center comes out clean.

Dessa's Pesto Presto

This recipe is great when basil is plentiful or you don't feel much like cooking. It can be tossed with cooked pasta or used as a garnish for grilled fish or chicken. Some cooks say that walnuts can be substituted for pine nuts, but that's never worked for me. It's also important to toast the pine nuts. I don't always bother, but those who *know* can tell the difference, though usually are too polite to mention it—except for Aunt Phoenix, of course!

Here's what you need:
   2 cups fresh basil leaves
   ⅓ cup pine nuts★
   3 cloves garlic, minced
   ½ cup freshly grated Parmesan or Romano cheese
   ½ cup virgin olive oil
   ¼ teaspoon salt or to taste
   ⅛ teaspoon pepper or to taste

   1.   Put the basil and pine nuts in a food processor and pulse until smooth.
   2.   Add the garlic and cheese and pulse several times more. Scrape down the sides of the processor bowl as needed.
   3.   Slowly pour in the olive oil in a steady stream while running the food processor. Scrape down the sides of the bowl as needed.
   4.   Season the sauce according to taste. If using it over pasta, leave it thick and add a little pasta cooking water. Add a bit more olive oil to make it into a loose paste over meats.

★There are several ways to toast pine nuts. Some folks roast them at 350 degrees F in the oven and watch them closely. I prefer to toast them in a dry stainless-steel or nonstick frying pan on top of the stove. Place the nuts in the pan and heat it to medium heat. Shake the hot pan regularly to toss the nuts so they won't burn on one side.

Don't miss any of Valerie Wilson Wesley's Odessa Jones mysteries . . .

A GLIMMER OF DEATH

Award-winning author Valerie Wilson Wesley launches a thrilling new mystery series set in New Jersey, featuring a multicultural cast, and starring a caterer-turned-Realtor with the gift of second sight . . .

In the first of a thrilling new series, one woman's extraordinary psychic gift plunges her already-troubled present into chaos—and puts her future in someone's deadly sights . . .

Until now, Odessa Jones's inherited ability to read emotions and foretell danger has protected her. But second sight didn't warn her she would soon be a widow—and about to lose her home and the catering business she's worked so hard to build. The only things keeping Dessa going are her love for baking and her sometimes-mellow cat, Juniper. Unfortunately, putting her life back together means taking a gig at an all-kinds-of-shady real estate firm run by volatile owner Charlie Risko . . .

Until Charlie is brutally killed—and Dessa's bullied coworker is arrested for murder. Dessa can't be sure who's guilty. But it doesn't take a psychic to discover that everyone from Charlie's much-abused staff to his long-suffering younger wife had multiple reasons to want him dead. And as Dessa follows a trail of lies through blackmail, dead-end clues, and corruption, she needs to see the truth fast—or a killer will bury her deep down with it.

Available from Kensington Publishing Corp. wherever books are sold.

A FATAL GLOW

Sometimes even good luck can mean bad fortune. For Odessa Jones—reluctant psychic, part-time caterer, full-time Realtor— an elegant affair turned deadly threatens her reputation, and her life . . .

Recently widowed Odessa Jones is sure the exclusive catering job she's scored from wealthy businessman Casey Osborne will propel her catering career into the big leagues. So when Dessa's pesky second sight warns her that Osborne is bad news, she ignores it. She wishes she hadn't when he drops dead at his brunch after sampling her homemade preserves. Osborne's death is declared a homicide. Dessa and the friends who helped her cook are considered suspects . . .

To clear her name and find the truth, Dessa delves into Casey Osborne's life. Everyone from his sinister business partner to his tormented ex-wife has reason to kill him—and the opportunity to do it. With the help of her *spirited* aunt, loyal coworkers and mischievous cat Juniper, she desperately searches for answers. Until a second murder leads Dessa down a frightening path filled with insidious hidden agendas—and someone poised to change her life forever.

Available from Kensington Publishing Corp. wherever books are sold.

Visit our website at
KensingtonBooks.com
to sign up for our newsletters, read
more from your favorite authors, see
books by series, view reading group
guides, and more!

Become a Part of Our
Between the Chapters Book Club
Community and Join the Conversation